Poppy Nichols

Assistant District Attorney

Poppy Nichols

Assistant District Attorney

Michael W Mitcham

All rights reserved. No part of this publication may be reproduced, distributed, or transmitted in any form or by any means, including photocopying, recording, or other electronic or mechanical methods, without the prior written permission of the author, except in the case of brief quotations embodied in critical reviews and certain other noncommercial uses permitted by copyright law. For permission requests, contact the author.

Any references to historical events, real people, or real places are used fictitiously. Names, characters, and places are products of the author's imagination.

Front cover art and book design by Rob Kosinski (RobKmusic.com). Back cover photo compliments of Rickie Smith, Digital Creator, Leesville, Louisiana.

Printed in the United States of America 2024

Copyright © 2024 Michael W. Mitcham
All rights reserved
ISBN: 9798882948541

OTHER BOOKS BY MICHAEL W. MITCHAM

Bird on a Wire
Charlotte MacHen: Angel on Fire
Charlotte MacHen: My Daughter's Keeper
Charlotte MacHen: The Yellow Scarf
Life on Old Sand Road – Short Stories from a Country Boy

SPECIAL THANKS

A special thank you to Marisa Zarzeski, who allowed me to use her likeness as *Poppy Nichols* on the cover of this book. Marisa is a practicing attorney in Tampa, Florida, and I count her as a good friend.

DEDICATION

FOR MY COUSIN, JEFF (LANNY) SIMMONS

Lanny spent the better part of his life with his family at *Trail's End* on the Sabine River in Evans, Louisiana. To Lanny, the Sabine was a blessing and a hardship. The old Sabine gives and takes life. But Lanny heard the music the waters of the Sabine played. I have walked down to the river many times with Lanny and heard what he heard: the beauty and serenity of the waters that have been flowing there for millenniums. On a recent visit, I found that the old river hadn't changed. It was still playing its song, and I'm sure Lanny was smiling because I knew he could still hear the music the Old Sabine was playing.

TABLE OF CONTENTS

PROLOGUE
    THE SABINE

CHAPTER 1
    THE RIVER

CHAPTER 2
    HEARTBREAK

CHAPTER 3
    SPORTSMAN'S PARADISE

CHAPTER 4
    THE DECISION

CHAPTER 5
    ON MY WAY

CHAPTER 6
    ON THE JOB

CHAPTER 7
    THE RIDE-ALONG

CHAPTER 8
    THE SWIMMING HOLE

CHAPTER 9
    THE O'SHEA RANCH

CHAPTER 10
    THE MOUNTED PATROL
CHAPTER 11
    NICK DURANT
CHAPTER 12
    THE WARRANT
CHAPTER 13
    THE ORCHESTRA
CHAPTER 14
    RIVER RAT
CHAPTER 15
    THE JOURNAL
CHAPTER 16
    DOUBLE DATE
CHAPTER 17
    POACHING
CHAPTER 18
    INCIDENT ON TEXAS HIGHWAY
CHAPTER 19
    THE FAMILIES
CHAPTER 20
    VISITING THE CRIME SCENE
CHAPTER 21

    DNA
CHAPTER 22
    ELIZABETH AND JERRY
CHAPTER 23
    THE WEEKEND
CHAPTER 24
    THE GOLD COINS
CHAPTER 25
    THE LAKE
CHAPTER 26
    A FAMILY MATTER
CHAPTER 27
    RAID IN CYPRESS COUNTY
CHAPTER 28
    PEACE ON THE SABINE?
CHAPTER 29
    HOW DO I SAY GOODBYE?
CHAPTER 30
    WOLF CREEK
CHAPTER 31
    LIFE AFTER DEATH
CHAPTER 32
    FOREVER AND EVER

CHAPTER 33
    A PROMISE FROM THE HEART
CHAPTER 34
    THE WEDDING VOWS
CHAPTER 35
    THE GIFT
CHAPTER 36
    OUR WISH FOR YOU
EPILOGUE – DAY OF RECKONING

PROLOGUE

THE SABINE

The Sabine River has run its course, dividing Louisiana and Texas for over twenty thousand years. It is five hundred and fifty-five miles long, and thirty-five of those river miles run along the western border of Vernon Parish. You need to know a bit about the Sabine River and its history to understand the land and its people.

For many years, the area in Vernon Parish, east of the river, was known as *'No-Man's-Land* or the *Neutral Strip*. Some people even called it the *Sabine Free State*. It was a lawless land in every sense of the word that belonged to no country after the *Louisiana Purchase*. Neither Spain nor the United States claimed it. The pioneers that settled this strip of land were rugged people. They carved a home out of this unforgiving wilderness and have held on to the land for generations. Through floods, droughts, snakes, mosquitos, and other hazards of the swamp, these people made a life for themselves in this harsh environment. This lawless area also attracted exiles, deserters, political refugees, fortune hunters, and outlaws. Highwaymen even organized and manned outposts to fleece travelers passing through this area. If you were a victim of a crime, it was up to you, as the victim, to get your justice. The settlers were a determined group of people who learned to co-exist under these circumstances.

Besides the Lewises and the McKays, at least fifty pioneer families live along the thirty-five miles of banks on the Sabine, and a hundred more families live a mile or more inland from the river. The Nichols, O'Sheas, Perkins, Machens, Simmons, Harveys, and Crafts are seven of those families. These people didn't tame the river; they bent and swayed with it. Many families lost loved ones to the river, but they all knew the hazards of working and living on its banks, and none of them would trade their way of life there. To them, the Sabine was not just a river. Its water was in their blood. For most of these families, there was no friction between them. The river had a way of draining your energy, which left little time for conflict. Most disagreements were worked out between families. There are always exceptions. The Lewis and McKay families were two of those exceptions. They were large families that would defend their part of the river to the death. It didn't help that they lived on opposite banks of the Sabine and hadn't gotten along for generations. This wasn't just a feud. It was a general hatred that went back over a hundred years. No one knew for sure how it started. Some say it was over logs, and others that it was over one side stealing cattle from the other and driving them across the Sabine from Texas to Louisiana or vice versa. However, no matter how it started, the bitterness only grew worse over the years.

Finding an unmanned boat floating in the river one late summer day was about to blow the lid off the Lewis and McKay hundred-year-old feud.

CHAPTER 1

THE RIVER

It was the summer solstice, and the days would get shorter after today. James was the youngest of the Lewis boys. And today, without his family's knowledge, he rose early to get out on the river before the day's heat made working unbearable. He knew from experience that the heat and humidity on the river this time of year could be stifling. He planned to get as many sinker logs out of the river as possible before noon. The hundred-and-fifty-year-old logs would fetch a reasonable amount, and young Lewis had a plan for the money once the logs were harvested and sold. The Lewis family owned over a half mile of the property along the Texas side of the Sabine River. Because the logs didn't pay allegiance to any particular part of the river, there had always been a dispute over the ownership of these logs. The McKay Clan owned property on the eastern bank of the river that called Louisiana home. Of course, this dispute was nothing new; it had been going on for over a hundred years. Each patriarch had threatened the other about taking logs out of the contested section of the river. And because of this dispute, the valuable logs remained in the river...until today. James had already winched two large logs out of the disputed area when he saw someone paddling a boat towards him. He squinted, trying to get a better look at the person in the arriving craft. Still, the glare from the morning sun reflecting off the water made it impossible at that distance to identify the boat's occupant. Then, as the boat got within a few feet of James, he recognized who it was.

James smiled and raised his arm to wave, then called out, "What are you doing out..."

But James couldn't finish the sentence before he saw the individual steering the boat alongside him, exposing his right hand with a large wooden oar. James' look of confusion didn't last long before he was clubbed over the head with the heavy oar. The aggressor panicked and reached into James' boat, feeling for a pulse. He was dead; his skull was crushed. The attacker grabbed and pulled the tow line of James' boat to the Louisiana side of the river. Not sure what to do next, he took out his cell phone and placed a call. After a short conversation, he struggled to carry James' body up a small bluff, where he dug a shallow grave. He rolled James into the hole and covered him with dirt and forest debris. Exhausted, the man returned to the river's edge and pushed James' boat out into the middle of the river. The man watched as the current did its job, floating the boat gently downstream. Next, he went to where the cable was attached to the two logs James had harvested. He took the cable and threw it over a stump protruding from the river where it could be seen. Then, he made his way to his boat and paddled off.

Chad Perkins had risen early this morning, wanting to get an early start fishing. Earlier this summer, he had found a couple of spots where the catfish were plentiful. As he got to the river, the sun was coming up, and the haze was rising over the slow-moving waters of the Sabine. Chad could almost smell autumn in the air. It had been one hot summer. As his small outboard motor chugged, he heard a Great Horned Owl hoot. He stopped beside a large, partially sunken sinker log as he readied his fishing rod. Looking up at the top of an old dead pine tree beyond the moss, he saw the owl staring down at him. Chad smiled as he baited his hook. He loved this peaceful time of day before anyone else was out on the river. He felt as if it belonged to him. He wanted to get in what might be his last morning of fishing before his last college semester started next week.

Chad looked toward the bank as he made his first cast. Once the bait was thrown, it immediately hung up on some brush on the Louisiana side of the river. "Damn," he muttered. He had no choice but to paddle his boat over to the brush so he could untangle the line from the shrub extending from the clay embankment. As he neared the bank, he saw something sticking out of the earth that gave him pause. Were his eyes playing tricks on him? What he saw looked like an arm protruding from the top of the riverbank. He knew he wasn't mistaken when he saw the familiar tattoo. Although the skin on the arm was withered and the tattoo faded, Chad knew who it was. The unmistakable image was of a lion's head with the word *TRODAIRE* beneath it. It was Gaelic for fighter. Chad also knew who the arm belonged to: the missing James Lewis. All of the Lewises had this same tattoo—it was their family crest. The past week, the river had been high, and apparently, the current had washed part of the bank away, exposing the body part. Chad maneuvered his boat to the high bank for a closer look. While still in the boat, he reached up with his pocket knife, slowly removed some soil from around the arm, and tried not to retch at the same time. Next, he reached into his vest pocket, removed his cell phone, and placed a call to the Vernon Parish Sheriff's Office to report the finding.

Being from Louisiana, Chad pulled his boat up on the bank on that side of the river. After securing his boat, he walked back to where he saw the arm. He confirmed he was staring down at a shallow grave when he saw human hair protruding from the dirt. Knowing this was a crime scene, he backed away carefully to avoid disturbing anything. Chad looked around to get his bearings and saw an old logging road that he knew led to the rear of Major McKay's horse barn. He walked up the road to wait for the responding deputies. He only had to wait for thirty minutes before two deputies arrived. Chad took them to the river bank, where the arm was exposed. The deputies called for a crime lab so they could begin the grim task of unearthing the body.

Anyone who grew up within a ten-mile radius of this river knew its history and the history of the river dwellers on each side. The Rufus Lewis Family owned three hundred and fifty acres on the Texas side of the river for over a century. The current patriarch of the family was an older, heavyset man with a permanent scowl between his brows. He had a curly brown beard and a very short temper. He cast an impressive shadow at six feet two inches, two hundred eighty pounds with a large girth. He was undoubtedly a man to be reckoned with. It was known that when he got angry with one of his workers, he would pull his .44 magnum pistol and fire it into the end of a log to get their attention. Nobody messed with Rufus. That included his six grown sons living on the property and two teenage daughters living with him and his wife, Norma. Like generations before him, Rufus Lewis made his living in the cutthroat logging, lumber, and cattle business.

Emmitt McKay, another pioneer everyone knew as the Major, lived on the Louisiana side of this great river. His family had made this land their home for generations. It was said that

Major's great-grandfather came down the river in a raft with not much more than the shirt on his back. When his raft hit a sandbar and came apart, it started sinking. It was settled—this would become his homestead. For as long as anyone could remember, there had been a McKay on the eastern bank of the Sabine. His land holdings included an impressive five hundred acres, with most of this land on the river. Land which was quite fertile because whenever the river overflowed, it washed volumes of topsoil onto the Major's property. He was also involved in cypress and pine timber production and cultivating hay and cotton fields. Emmitt was more cerebral than Rufus Lewis, but he was very opinionated. His stature was more diminutive than Rufus, but anyone who knew him would tell you he was just as dangerous. McKay had five grown sons, but only three lived on the river property, along with his twenty-year-old daughter, Bonnie Blue, and his educated and very proper wife, Margo. The other two boys lived in the community. Once they had married and started a family, their wives let them know that the river life wasn't what they wanted for their young families.

It had been a few weeks since Lewis' youngest son went missing while pulling sinker logs out of the Sabine. When his boat was found, there were no signs of foul play. It was assumed that he had been drinking and had accidentally fallen out of the boat and drowned. Some speculated that the river had washed him downstream. That assumption alone didn't keep the locals from concocting their own theories about what could have happened. It was no secret that Rufus and the Major intensely disliked each other. Calling it a dislike might be a misnomer. There was no love lost between them. This feud that went back over a hundred years, along with James' disappearance, only stoked this fire. The communities on both sides of the river were taking a position and placing blame, which fueled the hatred between the two families. But people on both sides of the river turned out to look for James Lewis. That included McKay and his sons, Cypress County, Texas Sheriff Mitchell Newman, and Vernon Parish, Louisiana Sheriff Bobby Craft. Hundreds of man-hours were spent looking for the young man, and the river was dragged with nets. They came up empty-handed. There was talk of a funeral but the Lewises wouldn't hear of it. Rufus Lewis made it clear that there would be no services for James because there was no proof that he was deceased. This was a heavy burden on his mother, who hoped her youngest son would walk through the door any day now. But all that would change today, on a remote eastern bank of the Sabine River. Soon, they would sing *You Raise Me Up* for young James at the Burr Ferry Community Church.

CHAPTER 2

HEARTBREAK

Bonnie Blue McKay was sitting on a couch in the family courtyard with her mother when her brother Jack came rushing in.

"Did you hear? They found James Lewis' body buried on the banks of the Sabine. His grave was on the northwest section of our property," Jack said, out of breath.

"Does your father know?" Margo, the matriarch of the family, asked.

"Don't know," Jack answered.

Before they could enter the Major's office, he came walking out. They could tell from the look on his face that he was in a state of shock. He told them that Sheriff Craft had called and advised him of the discovery. He knew he would be a person of interest for two apparent reasons. First, the body was found on McKay land, and the second was the ongoing feud he and Rufus Lewis had been embroiled in for several years. The Major assured Bobby Craft that he sure as hell didn't kill James Lewis, and if he had, he wasn't stupid enough to bury him on his own property. Lord, with the trouble and violent disagreements they'd had over the years, he could only imagine what Rufus was thinking. If things were reversed, he would probably think the same thing. He looked up at his family and saw Bonnie Blue was shaking and crying. The family knew that Bonnie and James were friends despite the family feud, but this reaction surprised her family.

"Bonnie, I know you lost a friend, but why are you this upset?" Margo asked.

Bonnie looked at her mother, breathing shallowly as she tried to catch her breath. Margo handed her a tissue and asked again what was going on. She looked up at her mother and took a deep breath.

Hesitantly, she answered. "James and I got to know each other in the church's young adult group. At first, we were just friends, but our relationship grew. We hid that we've been a couple for a while now. We planned to get married. We had already spoken to Pastor Tilley, who agreed to perform the ceremony, but with one condition. James and I had to tell our parents first. We were going to do that as soon as James sold his logs."

The Major and Margo sat down and looked at each other.

"Emmitt, did you know about this?" Margo asked.

"Hell no. If I had, I would have put a stop to it. This makes matters even worse. Everyone will think I killed James because of his relationship with Bonnie." He turned to his daughter and asked. "Who knew about the two of you besides Pastor Tilley?"

"No one that I know of. We were very careful to meet where no one would see us. We even went to see the Pastor separately so we wouldn't be seen together. Promise me, Dad, that you didn't do this," Bonnie said to her father.

"I wouldn't have harmed a hair on that boy's head. My feud is with his father, not him. But Rufus won't believe it. Jack, round up your brothers. Rufus will come with his boys, and we have to be ready."

"Does Sheriff Craft have any idea who did this?" Margo asked.

"No, not yet anyway. But if Rufus' bunch comes down the road to the house, we will have to call Bobby before we light 'em up. That's the best I can do," the Major said.

When Sheriff Mitchell Newman drove up to the Lewis home, Rufus was out the door before the Sheriff could get out of his vehicle. He stood on the front porch with his .44 magnum pistol strapped on. His wife, Norma, came out on the porch with her face buried in a kitchen towel, crying. Mitchell had hoped he would be the one to break the bad news, but someone had beaten him to it.

In a deep and loud voice, Rufus asked the Sheriff a question. "Do you know who murdered my boy, Mitchell?"

"No, Rufus, I don't, but Sheriff Craft in Vernon Parish is putting his full effort into apprehending the person who did it," Sheriff Newman said.

"Craft is a good man. I'll leave it up to him for now. But I better see some results soon. Is anyone going to check the owner of the property across the Sabine?" Rufus asked, pointing to the river's eastern bank, clearly referring to the Major.

"We're not jumping to any conclusions here, Rufus. Neither me nor Sheriff Craft are taking this lightly. Everyone will be checked out. Once we identify a suspect, Sheriff Craft has promised me he and the Vernon Parish District Attorney's office will make sure that all the legalities have been met and no mistakes are made."

"We may not have the fine education or gentile manners of some people around here, but I can tell you this place was not built and run by ignorant people. Anyone who thinks that is seriously lacking in judgment. My family and I are not to be trifled with. I hope you understand that, Mitchell."

In response, Newman cautioned Rufus and his family about taking matters into their own hands. After hearing the conversation with Sheriff Newman, Rufus' oldest son, Stewart, walked out onto the porch.

"Let me tell you, Sheriff. If we find the bastard that killed my brother, we will hang him from the Sabine River bridge," Stewart told him.

"Shut your mouth, boy," Rufus said in a loud and irritable voice, then walked over to him and slapped him open-handed across his face. The blow was so hard that it caused Stewart's head to spin violently to his shoulder. "Boy, I'll beat you to the ground. You don't speak for this family, and you won't do a damn thing unless I tell you. As long as I'm alive, you do what I say. Now get your ass back into the house," Rufus said, red-faced.

Stewart turned slowly and walked into the house with his head down.

"I'm sorry about that, Mitchell. That boy has no manners. His sensibilities are lacking," Rufus said in his deep, gravelly voice.

Sheriff Newman saw no reason to argue. He knew Rufus was a man of his word and would let law enforcement do their job. But only up to a point. Mitchell was sure that Rufus had a plan if they didn't find the killer quickly, and that plan would include violence. But he also knew that arresting the Lewis clan would be one hell of a job. Mitchell nodded to Rufus, got in his car, and drove away.

Stewart had good reason to be upset. He had suspicions about who killed his brother, but he couldn't speak up without causing more trouble for his family. If they knew what he and James had been doing when they weren't working the family business end of things, it would bring his father's wrath down on him big time. No, he would keep his mouth shut for now. But he couldn't help remembering the last time he and James had attended a meeting where James did his best to extricate himself from that criminal enterprise.

Nick Durant called the meeting to order after the sun went down in Bon Wier, Texas. He was well known around these parts by anyone and everyone unsavory. He ran a criminal organization that had started small but had grown over time. What with his contacts in the lumber and cattle business, he had no shortage of clientele ready to buy what he was selling. Whether it was cattle, horses, jewelry, or paintings, they lined up to do business with Nick. Stewart Lewis was among the attendees, along with his brother James.

James and Nick had known each other for over eighteen years— since they met at Burkeville Elementary School. They had started as classmates who barely said hello to each other, but they became quick friends once they found out they had a lot in common. The friendship lasted through high school, and survived football and girlfriends. So, when Nick approached James with an opportunity to make some extra cash, he said yes. Nick's enterprise had become very lucrative in a few short years. The way Nick explained it, all James had to do was sell a product for him that wasn't drugs. It sounded like fast cash for James' small role, which was to fence the property Nick's people appropriated. Well, the correct term would be misappropriated because what they were doing sure wasn't legal.

The extra money was good for part-time work, so he invited Stewart to join him. James and Stewart had no qualms about what they were doing. That is until James started dating a girl, and the relationship turned serious. She wasn't just any girl. Her name was Bonnie Blue McKay, and she was the Major's daughter, his father's fierce rival. She was a Christian girl, and they attended the same church. No one knew about their relationship except for Stewart because he had seen them kissing on a blanket along the riverbank. Except Stewart didn't know how serious it had become. If he had, he would have warned off James by reminding him that nothing good would come of the relationship because of the family feud. Being honest with himself, Stewart knew it wouldn't have done any good. James was smitten with Bonnie Blue. And he couldn't blame him. She was a petite blond with the deepest blue eyes, contrasting with James' dark brown hair, green eyes, and lean, tall body. She was worth Rufus Lewis' anger. James knew that Bonnie would not look kindly on his involvement in Nick's business enterprise, so he had been thinking about taking a step back and eventually getting out of it altogether. Knowing what Bonnie would say if she knew about his part-time job made him increasingly uneasy each day, and he liked the job less and less, regardless of the money. Oh, yeah, it would be hard to leave the money behind, but he would do it for Bonnie Blue.

Nick advised his pilferers who obtained the merchandise that they had successfully sold it all. They needed product, and he had new targets for everyone. James and his brother were part of the meeting because they had to know what the new product would be so they could begin offloading it once it was received. The Powell brothers, Harley and Marley, were part of the crew that obtained the goods for sale. Stewart kept his distance from them, as did James. Their reputation for violence was well known in Vernon Parish.

Everyone disbanded after Nick's associates received their assignments except for James, who hung back to speak to Nick.

"Nick, you got a minute? I need to speak to you," James said.

"Okay, but make it quick. I've got someplace to be."

"Nick, I'm thinking of leaving the organization. It's been great working together, and I can't complain about the money, that's for sure. I'm getting married soon, and I know this type of work will not sit well with my new bride. I wouldn't leave you in a bind. I can phase myself out while I train someone else to take over," James said.

Nick looked at him and laughed. That was not the response James was expecting. He had worked for Nick for four years, making him a lot of money. He thought their long relationship would mean something to Nick and that he would understand.

"How long have we known each other? Is it fourteen or fifteen years? You're not going anywhere, Jimbo. Working for me is a lifetime commitment. So, get your head straight and start planning on selling the next lot of merchandise," Nick told him.

"No, Nick, I have to quit. It would be best if you found someone else to do this work. Your enterprise and how it works is safe with me, but just don't come looking for me. Understand? Because it won't work out well for you," James said as he walked out the door.

Stewart, who was waiting for James, wasn't the only one to overhear what was supposed to be a private conversation. He spotted Harley and Marley nearby listening in, too. Knowing the mayhem these two caused everywhere they went, he couldn't help but wonder if they would try to use this information against James. Thinking that his brother had enough on his mind, Stewart decided to keep this to himself.

When James walked away, Nick was surprised at his push-back. He mumbled that he hadn't realized Jimbo had that much backbone. Stewart heard him calling for Max Bren to meet him outside the building. Max did odd jobs for Nick, one of which was enforcement of sorts. Max didn't have dazzling looks, but he didn't need them in his line of work. Most people called him slow, but not to his face. He was powerfully built and, most of all, very loyal to Nick because he gave Max a job when no one else would. He did Nick's bidding whenever it was required, no questions asked. Stewart heard

Nick give Max the assignment to persuade James to return and remain an integral part of the organization. He told Max to instill in James that there was no other choice. Nick made it obvious, in certain matters, that special handling was required. This was one of those matters.

James and Stewart headed home after the meeting, but Stewart could tell that James had other thoughts swirling through his head. He asked him if he wanted to talk it out. James told him that Nick's response to him wanting to move on was not what he had expected. Surely, their friendship over the years accounted for something. James hadn't missed the dangerous flicker in Nick's eyes. He couldn't help but think he should have handled it differently. But how? He wanted to be with Bonnie, and he couldn't be with Nick too. He couldn't embroil her in that type of setup. He wanted to marry her, and he needed to start their marriage with honesty. James knew if he told her what he had been doing for Nick these few years, she would look at him differently. Thinking of her, James picked up his phone and punched in her number. She answered on the first ring.

"Hi, honey. Not asleep yet?" James asked in a cheerful voice that didn't match his mood.

"Not yet, James, but why the late phone call? Is something wrong?" Bonnie asked.

"No, I just wanted to hear your voice, that's all," James said.

"That's so sweet. I was just lying here thinking of you, too."

Stewart knew his brother was too far gone in his love for Bonnie Blue. There was no turning back. But thinking how Rufus Lewis would take this news made him shiver. James had told him he had asked Bonnie several times to speak to her father about him. Bonnie had been trying to work up the courage, but she knew the bad blood between their fathers would be hard to overcome, if not impossible. But as Stewart listened in on James' side of the phone call, he knew she was assuring him she would speak with her father this week. Bonnie hoped she could keep that promise. As the only girl, their father treated her far better than the boys. They had a special relationship, but it only made speaking to him more difficult. James had told Stewart about meeting with Pastor Tilley and that he had said he would marry them, but they must tell their fathers first.

Paster Tilley knew that their marriage would bring war to the Sabine River without their fathers' blessing. He knew there was no putting out the fire once it was started. Since both families belonged to his church, he considered talking to them separately but decided it was best not to get involved in their business. Even though Pastor Tilley knew the couple cared deeply for each other and felt they were well-suited, he just wasn't sure this would work out.

CHAPTER 3

SPORTSMAN'S PARADISE

Poppy Nichols, at twenty-five, had grown into a striking young woman who towered over most men when she was wearing heels. Although she had a willowy build, don't mistake her graceful stature for weakness. Women of the Scottish bloodline had raised her, and they were as tough as they came. Poppy was taught to be strong, mentally and physically. There were no shrinking violets in this family. She was quite the athlete and more than capable of caring for herself. Her long dark hair draped over her shoulders matched her deep chocolate brown eyes, which appeared to be black when she was angry. It was best to get out of her way when you saw that look! Of course, that was a rarity; as most people would tell you, Poppy was a warm-hearted person who would give her last dollar to someone in need. Her Cupid's bow lips gave the appearance that she was always smiling. She showed an aptitude for learning at an early age, and it didn't hurt that she was a tenacious reader with criminal case history as her favorite subject. Her love of the law led her to work part-time at the Webb County Sheriff's Department in the detective division for two years. Grace's niece, Charlotte MacHen, has been the Sheriff there for almost twenty years. Poppy was able to squirrel away her earnings from the job to use towards law school. Referring to it as a job didn't reflect her true feelings— she absolutely loved all aspects of it. Poppy never liked second-place finishes, so no one was surprised that she completed her law degree at the top of her class at Mountain View University. Although she loved her adoptive mother, Grace, and her life in Webb County, she was ready to spread her wings and see the world. Well, not quite the whole world, just someplace else. She wasn't sure that she was prepared for a large metropolitan area and was also unsure that she wanted to exchange one small town for another. Poppy decided to throw caution to the wind and respond to job postings as close as Atlanta and as far away as Los Angeles. Most first interviews were done via Zoom or Skype in this social media and electronic world. She had made a 'shortlist' of what was important to her in her new career and planned to interview them while they thought they were interviewing her. Poppy was confident that the perfect job was just over the horizon, waiting for her.

"Poppy, graduation starts in an hour. Are you ready yet?" Grace asked.

"Yes, Mom, I'm just about done. All I need to do is put my shoes on," Poppy said as she hopped toward the door wearing one shoe.

Grace smiled as she looked at her daughter. Where has the time gone? She asked herself. It seemed like yesterday that she had taken a thirteen-year-old girl into her home and later adopted her. Poppy Nichols had been found alone and living in the mountains of northern Georgia. The poor girl had escaped kidnappers and decided to fend for herself on an unsuspecting farmer's property rather than return to her foster home. She survived on the eggs she took from his hen house and the fish she caught in the stream. This is where she was when the Webb County deputies found her. It was hard to believe that Poppy had progressed from an abandoned orphan to a law school graduate, and graduation day was here.

The trip to Mountain View University was a short fifteen-minute drive. As Grace drove, Poppy rode shotgun and had a big smile on her face. She rolled down the window of the truck, hung her head out, and with the wind blowing her hair straight back, she shouted at the top of her lungs, "Goodbye Webb County and hello world—you'd better look out for Poppy Nichols because she's on her way!"

Grace started blowing her truck horn and couldn't help but laugh. That was so like Poppy. When she first adopted her, she was a shy and skinny thirteen-year-old who had been neglected and unloved and pretty much tossed aside. Early in their relationship, Grace couldn't get more than a few feet away from Poppy because she thought Grace would abandon her, too. Now, she was a vibrant young woman ready to conquer the world.

Poppy tucked her head back into the truck, looked at Grace, smiled that contagious smile, and said, "I love you, Mom. You know I'm only planning to leave Webb County to see what else is out there, right?"

Grace nodded, but Poppy could see a few tears forming in the corner of her eyes. She hugged her mom as they drove to the graduation. She was going to miss her. This would always be home, but Poppy had to see what the rest of the world looked like. She knew that Grace understood that.

By the time they reached the University, both of them had big smiles on their faces. After all, this was a day for celebration. They both always knew the plan was for Poppy to relocate once she graduated. Besides, it gave Grace a reason to leave Webb County occasionally, as there would be lots of visits between them. Grace saw her niece and family as she inched into the parking space. Poppy noticed her adopted family at the same time. Charlotte MacHen, her husband Matt Hardt, and their daughters Rory, Alex, Hannah, and Harper Jean walked up to the car. This was turning into a graduation and family reunion combined. Charlotte and Matt's daughters lived in different cities, except for Harper Jean, who hadn't flown the coop yet at seventeen. In fact, these girls had encouraged her to look further afield for a job. They all loved Webb County, but after completing college, they were ready to try something new. So far, none of the girls had regretted their decisions. After hugs all around, Grace and family rushed inside the auditorium to take their seats while Poppy went into the staging room where the graduates were assembling. It seemed like only a few minutes later that Poppy was marching down the aisle to accept her diploma. As Poppy walked, she glanced over to where Grace was seated and smiled at her. Grace was so proud of her daughter that she was about to burst with pride.

Although Poppy had a new family, Grace knew she had always been curious about her birth parents. The feeling that they would have given her up always weighed heavily on her. She didn't know the circumstances, but Poppy had a sense in the back of her mind that it meant they didn't want her. She had been shuffled from one foster home to another since she was six months old. Heck, she didn't even know what state she was born in. Grace was the only mother she had ever known, and they loved each other unconditionally. Poppy would never do anything to make Grace think she wasn't happy. That's part of the reason she had never attempted to investigate where she came from. So, Grace's gift of a DNA test kit was a total surprise to her. It told her it was okay to be curious. She had followed the instructions that came with the kit and had mailed it off a couple of months ago, realizing that if no one closely related to her had also completed a test, she still might not know where she came from.

    Poppy studied as best she could for the bar exam while waiting for a response from her interviews. Each state has its own criteria for the exam, so she couldn't thoroughly study or apply for the test until she knew where she would be practicing. She had narrowed it down to four cities she thought she would enjoy living in, but Poppy cut the list to three after her online interviews. She just didn't get the proper vibe from the folks doing the Chicago interview. They were a bit too fast-paced for her style. But the deciding factor was the crime statistics she was able to access on the internet. Even though she had always liked studying crime, that didn't mean she wanted to be a victim of it. The remaining choices were San Diego, Miami, and a small town in a large Parish in Louisiana. The one that intrigued her the most was the Vernon Parish offer. Just the fact that they had parishes and not counties seemed like a sign to Poppy. She was looking for something different, and that might be the ticket.

    It surprised Poppy, but no one else, when Grace brought in the mail, and she had three offer letters. She had opened the first one with trembling fingers, read the offer, and put it aside to review the other two. Unsurprisingly, the starting salary in the two larger cities was higher than the offer from Vernon Parish, Louisiana. Poppy's goal wasn't about money. She was looking for an opportunity to go where she could make a difference and enjoy the people and the lifestyle the most. She sure had a lot to think about, including settling into an area and making it her new home. The deadlines to accept were all within a week's time. She looked to Grace for help deciding, but her mom told her she needed to make her own decision based on her research. Poppy re-read each offer, then pulled out her laptop and asked her good friend, *Google*, to help her out. Her plan was to make a list of pros and cons for each city. She had no idea that she would soon make a startling discovery that would sway her decision.

    It had been three days since Poppy had received her offer letters when Grace heard the train whistle go off on Poppy's laptop, indicating she had an email. Grace stuck her head out the door and told Poppy, who was sitting on the veranda reading, that she had mail.
    Poppy closed her book, went inside, and opened her laptop. While browsing her emails, Poppy saw a response from the DNA testing company regarding the kit she had sent off. She hesitated before opening it, not knowing what awaited her. Her thought was that just one click of the mouse would show her something exciting or possibly open Pandora's Box. Her mind made up, she clicked on the email and followed the link. What she saw made tears well up in her eyes–she had cousins, lots of them. Opening each link, she discovered several were in Texas and Louisiana. As she dug deeper into each relative's profile, their hometown of Leesville, Vernon Parish, Louisiana,

jumped out at her. Poppy thought this had to be a sign from God. She quickly grabbed the job offer letter from Vernon Parish and re-read it. It had been signed by the District Attorney, Timothy O'Connor, and she noticed for the first time that he had penned a personal note along with the job offer. It wasn't what he said in the letter, but just the fact that he had taken the time out of his busy day to reach out to her himself to say he hoped she would accept their offer and commented that he thought she would like it there in *Sportsman's Paradise*. Poppy had already discovered that Vernon Parish was on Louisiana's western border, separated from Texas by the Sabine River. Although it seemed far from the only home she had ever known, it was certainly closer than San Diego or Miami. Besides, she had family there! She just hadn't met any of them yet. Pretty sure she had made up her mind, she wanted to review what she had learned with her mother. Poppy just knew that this was the right move.

CHAPTER 4

THE DECISION

Poppy sat for a minute, just staring at her computer screen. She looked closely at every picture as she clicked on the profile of each relative. Then, she blew the images up to get a better look. Some of the relatives had a strong resemblance to her. For a moment, she was overwhelmed and found it hard to comprehend all of this new information. She sat back and thought for a minute. Did these family members even know she existed? If they did, why hadn't they reached out? Were her parents estranged from their families, and if so, why? Would they want to hear from her? She had so many questions. Now, this feeling of euphoria was turning to anger.

Leaning over Poppy's shoulder and looking at the screen, Grace commented. "Look, honey, at how many blood relatives you have. The genealogy map shows several of your cousins live in Louisiana. Here is a first cousin named Elizabeth Weaver, and you're in the same age range. Here's two aunts and an uncle that are closely related to you," Grace said excitedly.

"Mom, should I send them a message?"

"Why don't you start with your first cousin, Elizabeth Weaver? You can't get any closer than that. I bet she can tell you where you fit into the family dynamics. Send her a message introducing yourself, but don't get too personal," Grace said.

Thinking that was a good idea, Poppy sent a brief message to her until now, unknown cousin, with basic information about herself. She wondered if she would get a response. After all, her family had twenty-five years to look for her, so maybe they weren't interested.

Elizabeth Weaver was similar in age to Poppy, having been born in 1997—the same year twenty tornadoes touched down in and around her hometown of Dallas. She came into the world with as much gusto as the winds from the storm, which caused her parents to believe their daughter would be hell to reckon with one day. And she proved them right! Elizabeth grew up on a small ranch with horses and a few cattle. A land where barbecue and rodeos were a way of life. She was considered to be a tomboy by most who knew her. But they always clarified that by saying she was a 'stylish tomboy'. She loved shopping for clothes, especially fancy dresses. And each dress had to have a pair of high heels to go with it. At five-foot-nine with long blond hair flowing down her back and blue eyes framed with long eyelashes, Elizabeth was never at a loss for a date to a school dance—prom, homecoming, sweetheart dances. You name it! Her Texas drawl drew in the boys like honey attracts bees. When she wasn't playing dress-up, Elizabeth could be found on a basketball or volleyball court or a softball field at her high school alma mater, Richland Collegiate High School in Plano. She was not only an honor student there, but she excelled in sports. So much so that she received scholarship offers for two of those sports, but her future interests were more in scholastics. No one was surprised when Elizabeth received an academic scholarship to Texas Christian University. And they equally weren't surprised when she graduated from TCU at the top of her class with a degree in Criminology. Upon graduation, she was hired by the U.S. Marshall Service and was stationed in the Dallas area for the first two years, where she gained valuable training. Being close to family was nice, but Elizabeth wanted to see other parts of the country and put in for a transfer. She landed a position with the Western District of Louisiana, headquartered in Shreveport. She was assigned to Leesville, Louisiana, and stationed at the Vernon Parish Sheriff's Office. When she first received her assignment, it hadn't been her idea of seeing the world! But after a year on the job, she loved the area and appreciated the small-town atmosphere surrounding her. It was nice to soak in the folksiness of the people compared to the fast pace she had grown up with in Dallas.

Poppy heard her laptop make a train whistle noise an hour later, indicating she had a message. She opened it up and was surprised that her cousin, Elizabeth, had already responded. Poppy held her breath and then clicked the key to open it. Then she began to read.

Oh, my gosh, Poppy, what a pleasant surprise! When I read your message, I immediately asked my mom if she knew about you. Mom had no idea you survived. She told me that her brother, Louis, was in his twenties when he left home and didn't keep in touch with his family. We didn't learn until a few years ago that he and his wife, Abby, had died in a car accident. It was assumed their child died in the accident with them. That's why you could have knocked me over when I got your email. I am so anxious to talk to you. After all, we have twenty-five years to catch up on. I'm including my cell number with this message, hoping you will call. Excited to hear from you soon.
Your cousin
Elizabeth

Poppy immediately reached for the phone and called Elizabeth. They talked for over an hour, sharing bits and pieces of their lives. They were surprised at how much they had in common. While speaking with Elizabeth, she learned that although Dallas was her hometown, she lived in Leesville, Louisiana. She had accepted a transfer there with the U.S. Marshal Service about a year ago, not only because she liked the area but because she had relatives there—oodles and oodles of them. When Poppy heard that, she believed she had made her decision. She was going to accept the job in Vernon Parish. She wanted to share this news with Grace first. She would call Elizabeth back and let her know later in the week once she had all the moving parts in place. She hoped her cousin was as excited as she was. When she hung up the phone, she went in search of Grace.

"Mom, I've spoken to my first cousin, Elizabeth. I still can't believe I found her; she filled in some huge gaps for me. No one in the family even knew about me because my parents died in an accident, and their families thought I had perished, too. I'm having trouble understanding why the authorities at the time never tried to place me with family. I know it's been several years, but it's a mystery I would like to solve, and it's possible Elizabeth can help me. Can you believe that she is living and working in Vernon Parish? She's a U.S. Deputy Marshall and works closely with the District Attorney's office. After talking to my cousin, I've made up my mind. I'm taking the job there. It sounds so strange to be able to say 'my cousin'. She encouraged me to accept the job there and has never met me. And she told me that I have a lot of relatives there who will all be excited to meet me. Elizabeth's actual words were that you couldn't swing a cat in Vernon Parish without hitting a relative. Will you go with me, Mom, and help me get settled? I almost want to pinch myself to see if I wake up."

Grace was so excited for Poppy but couldn't help feeling a bit of jealousy. She never had to share Poppy before, but now she had what sounded like an extensive family. Grace had trouble getting the words out, but finally, she was able to speak. "Sure, sweetheart, I'll help you move and keep you company on the trip." It was finally setting in; Poppy was leaving home. Grace took a deep breath and looked at her daughter while she tried to hold back tears. She wasn't very successful because as hard as she tried, the tears came, and they wouldn't stop.

Poppy held on to the only mother she'd ever known, just as Grace used to hold on to her when she was a frightened little girl. She knew this would be hard for her mom because it was hard for her, too.

Grace wanted to do something extraordinary for Poppy for graduation but wasn't sure what to buy her. After all, you only graduate from Law School once. After Poppy decided to accept a job out of state, heck, almost halfway across the country, she knew the perfect gift. Poppy had been driving an old truck in high school and all through college. They kept it maintained, and it appeared safe, but it had the miles on it for sure. If Poppy agreed, she was going to buy her a new one. She considered it a gift to both of them. Poppy would love a new truck, and Grace would feel relaxed knowing she had a safe ride while living far from home. The next day, the two of them were at a truck dealership, and Poppy picked out a red pickup truck with black wheels. She wore a smile from ear to ear all the way home!

CHAPTER 5

ON MY WAY

There were still a few days before Poppy had to leave, and Grace intended to make the most of it. She promised herself that there would be no tears. They were going to enjoy the remaining days. She helped Poppy decide what to take with her and helped her pack for the trip. The plan was for Grace to drive with her to Louisiana, stay a few days to help her get settled in, and then fly back home.

It was evening when Grace walked onto the veranda and sat on the big porch swing. The cool evening air felt good on her face. Soon, Poppy came out with a light shawl and wrapped it around her, then laid her head on her mother's shoulder like she had done many times before when she was younger. She knew seeing her go would be difficult for her mom, especially with her new job being so far away. She would miss her, too. Poppy lifted her head and kissed her mother's cheek.

"I'm going to be alright, Poppy," Grace said with a smile.

"I know you are, Mom," Poppy answered.

Then they sat quietly, arm in arm, watching the moon rise over the mountains.

Grace looked at the clock for a second time after the alarm went off. Yes, it was five o'clock, and it was time to get up. What an emotional day this was going to be. Poppy was the only child that had ever called her mom. Although Grace had many opportunities to get married, she never found the right man, so there were no children—until Poppy. She looked in the mirror, groaned, and went to her daughter's room.

"Wake up, honey. We have to get ready. We leave in an hour."

Poppy opened her eyes and looked at her mother. Realizing this was it, moving day, she threw her arms around Grace's neck and held her tight. Grace's heart was breaking, but she knew she had to let Poppy go. Grace gently broke away from the embrace, walked back into her room, took off her nightgown, walked into the shower, and cried. She thought of a million ways that Poppy could stay. Poppy could be an attorney somewhere close to home, like Webb, Baker, or

Walker Counties. Or she could continue to work for Charlotte at the Webb County Sheriff's Office. But she knew in her heart Poppy had to go out into the world and make her way. Especially now that she had found her blood relatives.

"Mom, I'm ready," Poppy said loudly from her room.
Grace loved the word, Mom. She loved being addressed that way, and she was going to miss it.
"Good, I'm almost done. Get some breakfast. I've fixed your favorites," Grace replied.
Poppy could smell the food that her mom had prepared. Pancakes and smoked bacon—she couldn't get enough of it. That's what her mother has prepared for her every Saturday morning for years. They sat down and ate together, not saying a word. Each knew that they would both start weeping if a word was spoken. They just looked at each other, smiled, and ate. Poppy wondered if anyone would cook her this hearty of a breakfast once she arrived in Louisiana.

Poppy's new truck was packed and ready to go. Grace looked at Poppy and winked.
"Let's hit the road," Grace said with a smile.
Poppy smiled back at her and started the truck. With the truck pointed toward the interstate, she looked back in the rearview mirror and stared for a moment. She could see the only home she had ever known getting smaller in the mirror as she drove away. Reality hit her as she made the right turn onto

the highway. She was leaving her picturesque farm and soon her mother. Poppy and Grace looked at each other at the same time. Without saying a word, Grace reached into her purse and handed Poppy a tissue. She took the tissue, placed it over her nose, and blew—just like she had done as a child.

  Poppy and Grace reached their destination early Monday morning. They were thankful that it had been an uneventful trip and that the good Lord had provided lots of landscape for them to look at as they drove. Grace had gone online and booked a Bed and Breakfast for Poppy for a month until she could find an apartment to rent. It was downtown and close to Poppy's new job. She could walk to work if the weather permitted. As they drove down Third Street, Grace pointed to a modern-looking building with large black lettering on the front. It read: Vernon Parish District Attorney's Office, Timothy O'Connor, District Attorney. According to the GPS, the B&B was only two short blocks away.
  "This looks like a nice little town, Mom. It reminds me of home."
  "I like it too, but I wish it weren't so far from Georgia." Grace regretted her words as soon as they were out of her mouth. The last thing she wanted to do was to make Poppy feel bad about her choice. She quickly changed the subject. "Oh, look, there's the B&B just ahead."

Poppy parked in front of the building that would be her home for the next month. It was an attractive older home that had been well cared for. She and Grace walked inside to register and were met by an older woman with a pleasant smile.

"You must be Poppy Nichols," the woman said.

"Yes, I am. How did you know? Am I your only guest?" Poppy asked with a smile.

"No, hon, just a good guess. I usually know just about everything that goes on in Leesville and the rest of Vernon Parish, for that matter. I heard you'll be working for Tim at the District Attorney's office. Don't know if you've met him yet. If you had, you might have seen the resemblance," the woman said with a chuckle.

Poppy looked back at her with a puzzled look.

"Oh, since you're not from around here, you wouldn't know this, but he's my nephew—my sister's boy. By the way, my name is Olive. I live downstairs here. If you need anything, just knock on the door. Also, my phone number is taped on the inside of your room door. Don't worry about the time if you need to call because I'm a light sleeper."

After checking in, Grace and Poppy returned to the truck and grabbed their bags. Poppy couldn't help but think that the people here had a lot in common with folks in Webb County. There wasn't much that went on in town that they didn't know.

"Mom, do you think I should call my cousin Elizabeth and tell her I'm in town?"

"Sure, can't hurt. I'm sure she is just as anxious to meet you as you are to make her acquaintance."

Poppy picked up her phone and dialed Elizabeth's number. When Elizabeth saw the number on her caller ID, she immediately answered. She had been anxiously waiting for this call. She was so excited that Poppy and her mother were here in Leesville. As they made plans to meet for dinner, Elizabeth knew the minutes would drag by before she met her cousin in the flesh. Just think, they didn't even know the other existed a short time ago!

"If you like Mexican food, there is a great place down the street from your B&B called the Gringo Biscuit. I can meet you there," Elizabeth said.

Poppy shared the plans with Grace, who immediately nodded. They arranged to meet Elizabeth at six o'clock.

Over dinner, they got to know each other better. Oh, yes, they had talked often after finding each other, but it was surprising how much more there was to learn. Elizabeth had grown up in Farmers Branch, an area outside of Dallas. Tired of city life, she had jumped at the chance when a position came open in the district that covered Vernon Parish. Although she, like Poppy, had many relatives in and around Leesville, she had never lived there and knew little about it before relocating. Grace sipped a glass of wine while listening to their conversation. She learned that Poppy's father and Elizabeth's mother were brother and sister who had lost touch with each other. Meeting Elizabeth and hearing her speak about family made Grace more comfortable leaving Poppy in this city, which was unbeknownst to them just a few short months ago. Yes, she thought Poppy was going to settle in well here.

Elizabeth explained to Grace and Poppy that she had contacted her mother and asked how was it that she had a close cousin and had never known about her. According to Elizabeth's mother, it was due to her brother's estrangement from the family. When Poppy's father, Louis Nichols, left, he cut off all contact. She had already shared this information with Poppy in their first phone call, but it was essential to Elizabeth for Poppy to know that they would have taken her in if they had known she existed.

"I understand Elizabeth. If only my father had kept in touch with his family, maybe the first thirteen years wouldn't have been so tough on me. It's not your family's fault, but I was shuttled from one foster home to another. As the years went by, I felt no one wanted me. I couldn't figure out what was wrong with me. I wasn't an unruly child, but for some reason, no one chose to adopt me. That is until Grace MacDonald stepped in and brought me home to live with her. It was love at first sight for both of us. At least, I think it was because she chose me. She has been the best mother a girl could ask for." Poppy turned and looked at Grace and smiled. "I love you, Mom."

Grace looked back at Poppy and squeezed her hand. Poppy could see tears glistening in her eyes. She knew it was time to change the subject.

"So, Elizabeth, how long have you been with the Marshal's Service?" Poppy asked.

"It will be three years next month, and I love everything about it. How about you? You recently graduated, right?"

"Yes, I graduated from law school about three months ago and have been working for my cousin, Charlotte MacHen, the Sheriff of Webb County, Georgia."

"I've heard of her. Rumor has it she is one of the toughest Sheriffs in the country," Elizabeth said with a laugh.

"Not one of the toughest. She is the toughest. No one wants to tangle with her," Poppy said with a smile.

They talked for hours, but tomorrow was a work day, and they needed their rest. In fact, it would be Poppy's first day at her new job. They said goodnight to Elizabeth and left the Gringo Biscuit, heading back to the B&B. As they walked, there was no talking. They just enjoyed the quiet of the town, with the only sound being the occasional chirp of a bird. The street lights were dim, and the air was clean and fresh, with the pleasant smell of a Magnolia tree in the breeze. Poppy put her arms around Grace's shoulder and kissed her cheek.

"Mom, I think I'm going to like it here."

Grace looked at her and nodded. She knew Poppy would be happy here. From the time they had arrived, she was in her element. Leesville, Louisiana, fit Poppy like a glove. She could see and feel it—this would be Poppy's new home. This made Grace sad because she knew she would miss her. They had been together for twelve years now, and it was going to be difficult to adjust. But if Poppy was happy, then Grace was happy. She just wanted the right fit for Poppy. After all, that's what love is all about.

CHAPTER 6

ON THE JOB

Poppy had set her alarm for five a.m. She wanted plenty of time to prepare for her first day at her new job. She resisted the urge to hit the snooze button when the alarm jarred her awake. Instead, she turned it off, sat up in bed, and yawned. She glanced over to Grace's bed, hoping she hadn't disturbed her sleep, but the bed was made up, and Grace wasn't there. It would be just like her mom to get up early and go for a walk. After all, she was accustomed to rising with the rooster, having lived on a farm most of her life. Poppy got up, grabbed a terry-clothed robe, and headed for the shower. Her timing was perfect; just as she exited the shower, Grace entered their room with breakfast from downstairs.

"What do you have there, Mom?"

"It seems Olive is quite the cook. We have pancakes, bacon, blueberry muffins, coffee, and Louisiana cane syrup. What do you think?" Grace asked.

"I think my worry about getting a hearty breakfast once I arrived in Louisiana certainly wasn't warranted. This looks great." Looking over at her mom, she realized she might have hurt her feelings, adding, "But no one cooks a breakfast like you cook a breakfast. I will still miss our weekend meals and, of course, the company."

Poppy ate while the food was hot, then dressed in the clothes she had laid out the night before. She wanted to make a good impression, so she had chosen a navy blue suit with a pencil skirt and heels low enough not to hurt her feet on the short walk to the office. Poppy wanted to absorb the sights and smells of downtown Leesville on her way to work and chose walking as her mode of transportation. She knew that Vernon Parish was a large area spread over several miles, and she would have plenty of opportunity to explore it in her truck.

She walked into the District Attorney's office fifteen minutes early, wearing her business suit and carrying a fancy briefcase. Approaching the receptionist in the lobby, she told her she was the new Assistant District Attorney.

In return, she received a warm smile from the girl sitting behind the desk, who told her that her name was Tenley and she would show her around and introduce her to her teammates.

As Poppy followed Tenley, she noticed that everyone was dressed casually. All the attorneys were wearing jeans and cowboy boots. This included the lone woman ADA who had upped her look with a large belt buckle and a cropped short-sleeved blouse. Poppy noticed a blond male standing by the copy machine at the back of the room. Tenley introduced her to him first.

"This handsome rascal is Jerry Lambert, Chief Investigator for the District Attorney," Tenley said.

Jerry turned and gave her his electrifying smile. Poppy returned the smile and thought to herself that he was very good-looking.

"Nice to meet you, Poppy. Someone should have told you that we dress casually around here. When we go to court, we spruce up our look. That is, we put on a tie. You might want to leave the suit at home tomorrow; I'm sure you'll be way more comfortable," Jerry said, winking at her.

Jerry was known as a bit of a jokester, but he was loved by all, especially the women. At just under six feet tall, with curly blond hair, blue eyes, and an infectious smile, he had a muscular build that most guys envied. His permanent tan almost made him look out of place. Like he should be surfing in California. When Jerry graduated from high school, he thought his future aspirations leaned toward the law, so he applied to and was accepted at LSU Law School, where ninety percent of the graduates passed the bar exam on their first try. It wasn't until he finished law school and had taken and passed the exam that he realized he couldn't sit behind a desk all day. He still loved the law, though, so he applied for District Attorney Investigator positions in several cities. He immediately heard from ten different D.A. offices but chose Leesville, Louisiana, because of its proximity to Texas. Not that he had any immediate family left there now. His mother had passed away while he was at LSU. He had just celebrated his twenty-eighth birthday, and with another year gone by, he found himself reminiscing about birthdays past. Jerry's father, a marine, was killed off the coast of southern California when the Sea Knight helicopter he was in crashed. They never found the bodies. Jerry was just celebrating his second birthday when his mother got the news. He was raised in Waco, Texas, in a household comprised of just him and his mother, who never remarried. She couldn't bring herself to date other men—the sadness of losing her husband was too great. He wondered if that was why he had been hesitant to find someone and settle down. Well, his single existence could soon be changing. It was something he had been thinking about lately.

"Now, let's go meet the boss," Tenley said.
They walked down the hallway to an office with a large glass wall, where Poppy saw a man sitting behind a desk with his head bent down reading. The sign on the door read *Timothy*

O'Connor – District Attorney. Tenley knocked on the door, and the man looked up and motioned for them to come in.

O'Connor was a local product–born and raised in Vernon Parish. He first ran for District Attorney six years ago and won by a landslide. He wasn't sure if that was a testament to his qualifications or to the fact that he had kin all over the Parish. Tim was a husky guy, six feet tall, with short brown hair he wore in a crew cut style. He had been an outstanding tackle on the Leesville High School football team but left that behind when he went on to college. Like most practicing attorneys in Vernon Parish, he attended LSU law school. After all, considering any other college would have been considered treason by most folks around there. O'Connor had a pleasant demeanor, and he treated his staff well. They repaid him by showing up on time and professionally doing their jobs. After all, their actions reflected on him as District Attorney. Unlike the staff, he always wore a white shirt and tie to the office but added a blazer or sports jacket for court appearances.

"Tim, this is our new Assistant D.A., Poppy Nichols."
Timothy O'Connor stood up, walked around the desk, and shook Poppy's hand.
"Nice to meet you in person, Poppy. I hope you've gotten settled in. Have you had a chance to explore our corner of Louisiana yet?"

"No, Sir, not yet, just the downtown area, but I'm looking forward to it."

"Well, you will get to see Vernon Parish soon enough and get to know our law enforcement people too. I like to assign our new people to the Sheriff's Office for a month or two when they first get hired. You will be doing ride-alongs with them and observing their investigative technics so that you can see how we operate here. We're pretty easygoing and casual here in Vernon Parish, but we follow the letter of the law. I think you'll ease right in. There's a new U.S. Deputy Marshall with an office at the courthouse next to the Sheriff. You two probably should get acquainted. I think you will be collaborating quite a bit on some cases. Her name is Elizabeth Weaver."

"I have already met Elizabeth. As a matter of fact, she's my cousin," Poppy said.

"Now, I didn't see that coming," Tim said, smiling. "Your transition here from Georgia should be a relatively smooth one. I'll tell Sheriff Bobby Craft you'll be there shortly. Tenley will show you to your office, and the Sheriff will also set up a space for you there. Any questions so far?" Tim asked.

Poppy shook her head, and then Tenley led the way down the hall to show Poppy her new office. It was larger than she had expected, and she tried the chair out while taking in all that had happened so far this morning.

While Tenley helped her get her office set up, they chatted.

"So, Poppy, have you found a place to live in Vernon Parish yet?"

"No, I haven't even looked. I'm staying down the street at the B&B for the first month. I figured that would give me time to decide where I want to live."

"Oh, you're staying at Tim's aunt's place. Olive is good people," Tenley said.

"Let me ask you something, Tenley. Is everyone in Vernon Parish related?"

Tenley looked at her and grinned before answering, "Just about!"

As Tenley configured Poppy's computer, Jerry entered the office and asked if she was ready to walk over to the Vernon Parish Courthouse and the Sheriff's office to meet the Sheriff. She nodded, grabbed her purse, and followed him.

Several deputies were sitting around talking as they walked into the Sheriff's office. They looked up when they saw Poppy and Jerry.

"Hey Jerry, I didn't know this was bring your sister to work day," one deputy said, laughing.

"Oh, you might regret that comment, Tommy. She's the new Assistant D.A., and she's the one that will be monitoring your work," Jerry answered.

"Oh, damn, excuse me, Ma'am," Tommy said, smiling.

"Okay, let me get your attention fellows. This is Poppy Nichols. She will be working with you off and on for the next couple of months. I understand she is extremely proficient with a firearm and more than capable of self-defense. In other words, she might make some of you look like pansies," Jerry said, smiling and pointing at the deputies.

As Poppy was getting acquainted, Elizabeth came in, and all eyes turned to her. Elizabeth saw their eyes feasting on Poppy. They did the same thing when she first arrived, but she set them straight. A little bit of kidding was okay. After all, they typically worked together for more hours than they were at home. Just so they knew where to draw the line and that she deserved their respect.

"Can you believe it? We now have two beautiful ladies working out of the Sheriff's office," one deputy said.

"At ease, boys. This is my first cousin. Make her feel comfortable here," Elizabeth said with a smile. Then she turned to Poppy. "They are kind of rowdy, but they're all good guys."

"Okay, Jerry, I can take it from here. Follow me, Poppy; I got the Sheriff to give you the office next to mine."

Poppy walked into her second new office of the day and then turned to Elizabeth. "Wow, I've never felt so important. I've gone from working out of the break room at the Webb County Sheriff's office to having two of my own offices."

"Well, you'll find that we do things big here in Vernon Parish," Elizabeth said with a laugh.

CHAPTER 7

THE RIDE-ALONG

Poppy still hadn't met the Sheriff, Bobby Craft, and Elizabeth was going to remedy that. She walked Poppy down the hall to a large office with a big desk. Behind that desk sat Sheriff Craft. He immediately stood when they entered and offered his hand to Poppy. Elizabeth made a quick introduction and then excused herself so they could get acquainted.

Like most elected officials in Vernon Parish, Sheriff Craft was born and raised there. He was a stout man with large shoulders and big arms. Craft had penetrating, steely gray eyes that could put fear in any man that challenged him. He wasn't excessively tall, but his graying chestnut hair and baritone voice portrayed a commanding presence. There was no question when you had crossed Sheriff Craft. He had no problem letting you know. He dished out immediate attitude adjustments. He and District Attorney O'Connor played together on the offensive line of the Leesville High School football team. They had been friends since elementary school. Together, they made a formidable law-enforcement pair. They always seemed to be on the same page.

 After giving Poppy a quick 'lay of the land' speech, he asked her if she was up for a ride-along today with one of his deputies. Poppy jumped at the chance. She was anxious to get started and couldn't wait to see more of Vernon Parish. Craft liked her enthusiasm and inquired if she had brought a weapon. Poppy nodded and told him that she typically carried her Glock 9mm. Without raising an eyebrow, he told her she could carry it, but he wanted her to be range-certified by next week.

 Craft informed her that today's assignment would be a patrol area in the western part of Vernon Parish. It would stretch from the Sheriff's office in downtown Leesville to the Sabine River, about twenty-four miles to the west, straight to the Texas State Line.

 "That's a pretty big chunk of real estate," Poppy said.

 "That it is, Poppy, but we keep it under control. The people out this way, for the most part, are good, solid people, but every once in a while, one of them wants to kick up some dust, and that's when we step in."

Elizabeth returned with a deputy in tow before Poppy had left the office. "I have to go up to the northern part of the parish today with a couple of deputies. Tommy here is one of them—we're just waiting on Gene. We have a federal warrant for a fugitive close to the parish line. That'll be my day. So, I heard about your first day's assignment, Poppy. No matter who you draw for the ride-along, I think you'll learn a lot."

"That sounds dangerous. Just be careful out there, Elizabeth."

"It'll be a piece of cake, Poppy. You're gonna take care of me, right, Tommy? Now, where the hell is Gene? He's the real deal," Elizabeth said, laughing and looking at Tommy.

Tommy pasted a big grin on his face and gave Elizabeth a thumbs-up.

It was almost nine o'clock when the Sheriff stuck his head into Poppy's office and told her she would be riding with Deputy Donovan Moore. He was waiting for her in the Sheriff's Office parking lot. She would have no trouble singling him out as he was driving the only high-wheel SUV the Sheriff's department had. Poppy grabbed her briefcase and left the building. She spotted Donovan right away, and they shook hands. He unlocked the passenger door, telling her they could get acquainted on the long ride. Poppy climbed in, ready to start her first day as a Vernon Parish ADA.

"Well, Ms. Nichols, are you ready to see some of Louisiana?"

"Drive on Deputy Moore. Let's see what she looks like," Poppy said with a smile.

Deputy Donovan Moore was a tall, slim man, very lean, with short black hair combed straight back and hazel eyes. He had a pleasant smile and a congenial personality. But Poppy could tell after a brief conversation that he was not one to trifle with. He showed people respect and expected it in return.

Poppy and Moore were in the Evans community when a call came over the radio that shots were fired at deputies and a U.S. Deputy Marshall serving a warrant in the northern part of the parish.

"Donovan, are we going to take that call?" Poppy asked. "I'm sure that's my cousin, Elizabeth Weaver, up there."

"No, it's too far from us, and there are closer deputies that can respond quicker. We're forty-five minutes away, even with red lights and sirens blaring. Listening to the dispatcher, it sounds like there's already four units responding who are only five minutes out," Donovan said.

Poppy sat back in the seat and did what Donovan suggested. She paid attention to the dispatcher, praying that Elizabeth was safe. She heard the radio crackle.

"VP-10 to all units. U.S. Marshall Weaver has the suspect in custody, and there are no LEOs injured. They are en route to the hospital now to have the suspect examined before arriving at the jail. The fugitive sustained some injury while being taken down."

After that transmission by Deputy Tommy Jones, it seemed like every deputy's mic was clicking, which was a sign that the deputies were giving their approval of the outcome.

Poppy sat back in the seat and took a deep breath. She hadn't realized the adrenaline that was pumping through her. She looked at the ball-point pen she had been holding and noticed she had snapped it in two.

Moore looked over at her and saw how tense she was. Then he glanced at her left hand, where she had been holding the pen. She had cut her thumb where it had broken.

"Are you gonna be okay? There are some antiseptic wipes in the backseat for that hand," Moore said.

As Poppy reached for the wipes, she could see how concerned Moore was about her from his expression.

"Do you get used to this?" Poppy asked.

"No, never! Not ever. And you never want to get used to it," Moore said, looking straight ahead.

It was past noon when Moore stopped at a country store.

"You hungry?" Moore asked.

"Sure, I could eat some lunch."

Moore pulled into the store's parking area and said with a laugh, "This is the closest thing we have to a restaurant out here. I hope you like making your own sandwich."

"I think I can handle it," Poppy said, smiling.

After lunch, Moore took Poppy to Burr Ferry. "You see that bridge over there? The water flowing under it is the Sabine River, and the other side is Cypress County, Texas. That is Sheriff Mitchell Newman's County. He works with us a lot. Some people try to avoid justice by crossing that bridge. That hasn't worked out too well for them. Sheriff Newman, just like Craft, is a good man."

What Moore didn't mention was that there was a serious rivalry on the river between two families that had been going on for over a hundred years. One family lived on the Louisiana side, and the other resided on the Texas side. Most think it started with the recovery of sinker logs in the river. Each family had land that went to the bank of the Sabine. And each thought they owned all the logs in the river, forgetting that the logs had been in the river for years. Both families claimed the valuable commodity belonged to them. So much so that every time the families went into the river to harvest the timber, the other would shoot in the air close to them. So far, not one of them had been hit, but Moore, like most law enforcement, knew it was only a matter of time.

On the Texas side of the river was sixty-year-old Rufus Lewis, a burly Scot with a sour demeanor. His towering bulk, curly, caramel-colored beard, bushy hair, and thick eyebrows made him look intimidating. He lived on three hundred and fifty acres with his family, which included a wife, six sons, and two daughters. The Lewises made their living from cattle and timber. The way Rufus saw it was that anyone messing with the logs in the river was interfering with his ability to make a living.

On the Louisiana side of the Sabine was Emmitt McKay, the patriarch of the McKay clan. With his five hundred acres, he considered himself *King of the River*, so to speak, and he didn't allow anyone to take advantage of him. Never had, never would. He might have been smaller than Rufus Lewis, but he made up for it with more intellect and better judgment than Rufus. The Major was just under six feet tall with graying brown hair and bright blue eyes. His stature portrayed a professional presence. He chose his words carefully when he spoke, and they poured out like pure honey—that was his southern kicking in. He had a lean, wiry look and very little body fat. McKay had three grown sons living on the property, along with a twenty-year-old daughter and his wife. He was known on both sides of the river as The Major. No one quite remembered how he first got this name, but everyone knew to call him that. His family's business included hay and cotton fields along with cypress and pine timber production. Emmitt let no man infringe on the family's business on land or on the river.

Unbeknownst to Poppy at the time, she and Elizabeth were going to get very familiar with both families and both sides of the Sabine.

CHAPTER 8

THE SWIMMING HOLE

Poppy returned to the B&B only to find Grace missing. Figuring her mother was exploring on her own, she decided to change into something more comfortable. Grace came in the door with her arms full of shopping bags as Poppy was removing her clothes.

"Well, it looks like you've had a nice day. You didn't clean out all the shops on Third Street, did you?" Poppy asked with a smile.

"Not hardly, but some shops had locally crafted items that I couldn't pass up. I thought I'd do some early Christmas shopping," Grace replied.

"Show me what you bought, and I'll tell you about my day."

As Poppy shared her adventure of the ride-along, Grace opened bag after bag of beautiful handmade items and showed them to her. She tried her best to concentrate and not show her misgivings about Poppy's new job. She liked a good adventure herself, but what had her daughter gotten herself into? When Poppy said she wanted to be a lawyer, Grace hadn't pictured anything like this. And she reminded herself it was only her first day on the job. Grace had never been good at hiding her feelings, and Poppy immediately picked up on her apprehension. Changing the subject, she told her mother to freshen up because she was taking her to dinner at a place she heard the deputies talking about. If they were right, it served the best barbecue in the South.

She must have been sleeping soundly because she felt like her head had just hit the pillow when she heard the alarm clock. It was still dark outside when she slowly rose and yawned. Looking over at the other bed, she noticed the alarm had not awakened her mother. Dressed in yoga pants and a T-shirt, she went downstairs and grabbed two cups of coffee, biscuits, and homemade jelly. When she returned to the room, Grace was awake and dressed. Poppy extended her hand to her mother with one of the cups, and Grace took it willingly. She could tell by the look on her face that she was thinking her time here was almost up, and she would be going back to Georgia in a few days. Poppy knew her mother would miss her because she felt exactly the same.

It wasn't even eight a.m. when Poppy walked into the Sheriff's Department dressed way more casually than she had on her first day. As she said good morning to the deputies in the squad room, they couldn't help but tease her about her punctuality. Habits were hard to break, and as long as she could remember, she was always early for everything. She laughed with them and told them that at least she wasn't wearing a suit today. She went to her office, put her briefcase and purse down, and walked to Elizabeth's office.

"Good morning, cousin," Elizabeth said with a smile while reaching into a large bag beside her desk. She pulled out a loosely wrapped parcel that she handed to Poppy.

Poppy looked from the package to Elizabeth questioningly.

"Go ahead, open it," Elizabeth said.

Poppy slowly unwrapped the box and opened it. Inside was a brass desk plaque. She laid it down on her desk so she could read the inscription.

Justice:
God demands it
Victims cry for it
We in LAW ENFORCEMENT deliver it

Poppy looked at it, and after a long pause, she looked at Elizabeth. "Thank you for this. I love it and will always keep it with me."

"Anytime you're feeling discouraged, and you will believe me, just take a few deep breaths and remember those words. It will help you get your second wind."

Elizabeth told Poppy she had seen on the assignment board that Tommy Cain was her ride-along for today. Then she added. "Just an FYI, Poppy, Tommy is easy on the eyes, and he's not married."

Poppy laughed and asked, "Aren't you interested?"

Elizabeth hesitated before answering. "I've been seeing someone on the 'down low', Jerry Lambert. Since he works for the District Attorney, we thought we would keep it quiet—fat chance of that in Vernon Parish. We've heard some whispering, so we're going public with our relationship. Since his is a local position and mine is federal, there's no rule against it. We thought we wouldn't announce it until we were sure about each other. Thought it would be odd enough for us seeing each other every day if it didn't work out, never mind having everyone else looking at us. You know what I mean? He's kind of crazy, and I'm more serious, but I like him. He makes me laugh, and the fact that he's good-looking doesn't hurt. We kinda mesh," Elizabeth said.

"Yeah, I do, and I'm a bit jealous. I haven't met anyone that pulls my chain quite like that. Sounds like it's working out just fine," Poppy said with a smile.

"Look, I'm going to change your assignment for today and have you ride with me. If you're willing to give up a chance to ride with hottie Tommy. Are you okay with that?" Elizabeth asked.

"Sure, that's fine," Poppy said with a grin.

After grabbing a couple of coffees for the road, they got into Elizabeth's car and headed west on the Texas Highway. They had gone about fifteen miles when Elizabeth turned right onto a small paved parish road. She drove about two miles further and made a westerly turn on a wide white shell road. As they reached the end of the road, there stood a beautiful mansion-styled home with white columns in the front. Elizabeth stopped on the flagstone driveway in front of the house. She looked over at Poppy.

"This is the Major's house. Don't ask me why they call him Major. I've asked, and the answer I get is that that's the way it's always been. I think that means that no one alive really knows. His real name is Emmitt McKay, and he's gotten rich living off this land. About a hundred yards behind his house is the Sabine River, and the State of Texas is on the other side of that river. That Texas parcel of property is a tad smaller than this one, and it belongs to a nasty old bastard named Rufus Lewis. Now he's someone where you have to watch your back when you're around him. Oh, make no mistake. The Major is just as dangerous but a bit nicer about it. Those two haven't gotten along in over thirty-five years and damned if I know why. The Lewis and McKay families have been at odds for over a hundred years. That's another question the locals don't have an answer for. If things weren't bad enough already, about a month ago, old man Lewis' youngest son, James, who was missing, turned up dead and buried on the Major's property. The situation is at its boiling point right about now. Sheriff Newman over in Cypress County, Texas, and Sheriff Craft and I are trying to relieve some of that pressure so there's no explosion."

"How's that working?" Poppy asked.

"It's not," Elizabeth said.

Elizabeth looked toward the front of the house and saw Bonnie Blue walking toward them. Elizabeth had only known her briefly, but they bonded over Elizabeth's *city look*. Bonnie wanted to learn how to do her hair and makeup like the people she saw on T.V. Elizabeth was happy to show her in the sparse time they had shared together. She said hello to Bonnie Blue and introduced her to Poppy. After shaking hands with Poppy, Bonnie told them her dad wasn't home but invited them inside. Elizabeth only planned to stay for a minute since the object of her visit wasn't available. Poppy's jaw dropped when she saw the foyer that opened up like a rotunda. Bonnie then walked them through a large living room with French-style décor. She walked further with Elizabeth and Poppy, following her to the rear veranda covered with beautiful plants and wisteria vines. The furnishings outside were just as ornate as the ones on the inside.

Bonnie Blue asked the maid hovering around them to bring some iced tea. Within a few minutes, a tall, dark-haired woman came walking out. She had an elegant but old-world look about her and a polished demeanor.

"Hello, Elizabeth, who's your friend?" Margo asked in a soft southern drawl.

"Margo, this is my cousin, Poppy Nichols, the new Assistant District Attorney. She recently relocated here from Georgia. Poppy, this is Margo McKay."

"Nice to meet you, Poppy. How do you like our little corner of the world?"

"I haven't been here very long, Mrs. McKay, but so far, I love it. I think I'm going to fit right in here."

"Nichols is a big name here in Vernon Parish. I don't suppose you are related to the Louisiana branch of the family?" Margo asked.

"As a matter of fact, I am. In fact, it was a recent discovery." She didn't miss the look of surprise reflected on Margo's face.

"Well, it was nice meeting you, Poppy." And with that, Margo abruptly turned and walked away.

They continued their conversation with Bonnie Blue for a few more minutes as if Margo had not even stopped by. Poppy couldn't help but think that Bonnie's mother's behavior was not in keeping with her outward appearance. Surely, someone of her stature would have found a smoother way to exit their company. Elizabeth ended the conversation by telling

Bonnie they had to be on their way. They said their goodbyes and Elizabeth and Poppy returned to the car.

"That was a little strange," Poppy said. Did I say something to offend Mrs. McKay?"

"I don't think so. That's just Margo. She attended college at LSU and picked up her style there. The problem is, that was almost thirty years ago, and no one has had the nerve to tell her that the world has changed since then, and so has the fashion."

"Where are we going now?" Poppy asked.

"We are going to Pearl Creek, one of my favorite places."

"What's at Pearl Creek?" Poppy asked.

"It's not what's there. It's what we'll do when we get there—we're going skinny-dipping!" Elizabeth said shamelessly.

"You ARE kidding me, aren't you?" Poppy asked

"Nope, not at all. Sometimes, you just have to say, 'What the hell'. Besides, the place is beautiful. You're going to love it."

It was a short drive east on the Texas Highway, then an even shorter drive down a dirt road that abruptly stopped at a beautiful tree-lined creek. The trees formed a canopy over the water...water that flowed over pearl-white sand. Elizabeth stopped the car and started undressing with no modesty, throwing her clothes on the car's hood. She looked over at Poppy.

"Come on, get those clothes off, girl," Elizabeth shouted as she ran toward the water naked and jumped in.

Poppy was unsure, but she slowly removed her clothes and placed them on the hood. It felt like she was playing hooky for the first time in her life. At first, she did a slow walk to the water's edge, but after going just a few feet, she turned it into a full sprint. Once she reached the water, Poppy dove in headfirst. Straight into Pearl Creek in the buff! As the two of them were splashing around and talking, they noticed a man come riding up on a horse. He was tall and slim and wearing a cowboy hat. When he approached the water's edge, she noticed he looked like someone who had come straight out of central casting in a Hollywood production. As he got closer, they sunk deeper into the water until they were neck-deep.

"Good morning, ladies. I was looking for some strays. I don't suppose you have seen any?" He asked with a smile.

"No, we haven't seen any cattle today," Poppy said.

"Okay, thank you, ma'am." He turned his horse around to ride off, stopped, then turned around in the saddle and looked back at them.

"You ladies do know they call this Pearl Creek because you can see all the way to the pearly white bottom." He tipped his hat, turned around in the saddle, and rode off.

The girls looked down and realized the handsome stranger was right. The water was crystal clear from the surface down to the sandy bottom.

"Oh my God, I didn't even shave my legs this morning. Do you think he noticed?" Elizabeth asked, smiling while looking at Poppy.

"With his clear view of us in the creek, I doubt he was wasting time looking at your legs, Elizabeth."

Then, the two of them broke out laughing.

Once they were out of the creek, they dressed and headed back towards Leesville when Elizabeth asked. "Poppy, how would you like to stop by and visit some family? They don't live far from here?"

"Sure, I'm game. Who are they?" Poppy asked.

"Uncle Mark and Aunt Bessie Perkins. Aunt Bessie was a Nichols; she is our parent's great-aunt. The Nichols' name has been in Vernon Parish for over one hundred and sixty years. The family were pioneers of this parish. Mark and Bessie are getting older but still work the farm."

Elizabeth slowed the car down and turned down an old sand road. At the end of the lane were beautifully manicured fields and a well-kept home nestled under four ancient oak trees. As they drove up to the front gate, it was apparent that no one was home. Poppy sat and took in the scene. The farm looked as if it were out of a Norman Rockwell painting. She was astonished at how she had gone from an orphan with no known relatives to a place where she was virtually related to everyone. Poppy was surprised that she had relatives who had worked these lands for all those years.

After a few minutes, Elizabeth turned the car around and drove back to Leesville.

CHAPTER 9

THE O'SHEA RANCH

"Mom, it's time to get up. Your flight leaves in two hours, and we have a forty-five-minute drive to Alexandria Airport.

It was unusual for Grace not to be the first one up and dressed. She always woke Poppy in the morning. Grace sat up in bed, and her eyes rested on Poppy. Even though she knew this day would come, she had put it in the back of her mind. But, today, reality set in—she would be separated from her daughter for the first time in almost fourteen years.

"Okay, sweetie, I'll be ready in fifteen minutes. My bags are packed, and all I have to do is brush my teeth."

Within twenty minutes, they were on their way to the airport. While driving, Poppy occasionally looked over at her mother. She knew how hard it was for her to leave her behind, especially in a city neither of them had set foot in until a few days ago. Her mother had and would always be her hero; after all, she saved Poppy as a young girl. Having been brought up by this remarkable woman, she knew what she was capable of. Poppy would always be her mother's cheerleader.

When they arrived at the airport, Poppy parked and walked with Grace as far as security would let her. As she said goodbye, she had tears in her eyes. Poppy was holding back her own tears as best as she could. When it came time for Grace to head towards the departing gate, Poppy grabbed her mother and held her tight. The tears flowed freely from Poppy like never before. Today reminded her of when she was a frightened girl, and Grace would hold her and reassure her. Poppy felt everything would be okay because her mother would always be there. Both of them knew it would be a hard adjustment, but one that had to be made. Grace reminded her she needed to find a place to board her horse, Peggy McQue. Poppy assured her as soon as she made arrangements, she would send for Peggy.

Poppy stayed behind and watched her mother's flight leave. She sat for a minute and wiped her eyes. When she regained her composure, she went to her truck and started the trek back to Leesville. She couldn't help thinking this was the loneliest drive of her life.

Poppy didn't want to be alone in her room, so she drove to Elizabeth's apartment, hoping she was home. She was the closest family Poppy had nearby now that her mother had returned to Georgia. Elizabeth soothed her by telling her she felt the same way when she left her family behind and came to Leesville. After a bit of a pep talk from Elizabeth, Poppy dried her tears. After all, the only home she had ever known in northern Georgia was a short flight away. Starting today, Poppy had to begin setting down roots in Vernon Parish, her new home. Besides, it would keep her busy.

When Poppy asked Elizabeth if she knew of a good place to board her mare when she arrived, she could only think of one place.
"Come on, let's go for a drive," Elizabeth said.
"Where are we going?"
"To the only place that I know of that boards horses. The O'Shea Ranch out on Texas Highway west of Leesville," Elizabeth answered.

It was only a fifteen-minute drive to the ranch, and on the way, Elizabeth shared what she knew about the O'Shea's, which wasn't much. When she saw the ranch sign, Elizabeth turned down a wide white shell road that rambled over a brook and through some pine trees. She drove up to a large white two-story house. A short distance from the home was a large modern barn with corrals in the space to the rear of the barn. This one was one of the nicest barns Poppy had ever seen. It was almost nicer than some houses back home. They spotted a sign that read OFFICE and an arrow pointing towards a large door. Poppy tried the door, and it was unlocked, so she walked in. She first saw a display case filled with gold belt buckles. Next to it was a shelf that held several trophies. She spotted a few fancy saddles trimmed with silver that Poppy knew were only used in shows.

A tall, slim woman in her mid-thirties smiled and spoke to them as they walked in the door. "Good morning, ladies. Can I help you?"

"I hope so. I just relocated here from Georgia, and I'm looking for a place to board my palomino mare. I understand you board, and I was wondering if you had any room for her?"

"Oh, I bet you're Tim's new Assistant D.A.," the woman said. She saw the surprised look on Poppy's face. "We know everything that happens around here. You will get used to it after a while. It keeps people on their toes. Sometimes, it stops them from doing something they don't want all of Vernon Parish to talk about," Tammy said with a laugh. "By the way, I'm Tammy O'Shea. I didn't catch your name."

"I'm Poppy Nichols, and this is my cousin, Elizabeth Weaver."

"I know you came from Georgia, but is there any chance you're related to any of the Nichols from around here?"

"I am. I just haven't met any of them yet, except for Elizabeth." Seeing the quizzical look on Tammy's face, she explained. "I didn't know I had kin here until a couple of months ago. I did a DNA test and found Elizabeth, and from there, I've located several more cousins."

"Oh, those DNA tests are really popular these days. But they should come with a caution label that reads. 'You better be well prepared for what you might find'. I've heard of a few locals who found skeletons in their closets that they had no idea about. One person, who shall remain nameless, found so many skeletons he needed a walk-in closet to hide them all. But back to your original question. We have one vacancy right now, so we can accommodate you. Even if we didn't, I'd find a way to make room for a Nichols. Just let us know if you want us to handle the feed or if you want to handle your own feeding. We buy only timothy hay. All you need to do is fill out some paperwork and provide proof of your mare's shots being current, and you're ready to go."

Poppy wondered if Tammy's talk of DNA and skeletons was a cautionary tale for her. Time will tell, she thought. She liked the fact that Tammy was a straight shooter. You didn't have to guess what was on her mind. "I can take care of the paperwork right now, and I'll have my vet email you Peggy McQue's records. By the way, these trophies and belt buckles are quite impressive. Who's the accomplished rider?"

"Well, some belonged to my father, who was a bull rider. And some, my mother won. She was quite the barrel racer. Those trophies over there are my brother Kurt's. He's a champion roper and saddle bronc rider. If you followed the circuit, you might have heard of him. The saddles and most of the buckles are mine. I won them for barrel racing. I learned from the best, my mother. Unfortunately, both of my parents passed away a few years ago. After that, Kurt and I retired. Me from competition and him from the circuit. We run the ranch together now. I oversee the business, and he runs the day-to-day operations. If you have the time, I'd like to show you around. We're pretty proud of our setup here. You might even meet my brother. He was planning to mend some fencing last I spoke to him."

Poppy looked at Elizabeth, who nodded. "Sure, we'd like that. Might as well see who my Peggy McQue will be hanging out with."

They left the office and headed towards the barn. It was bigger than any barn that Poppy had seen before. Elizabeth was used to everything being bigger. After all, she was from Texas. Poppy counted sixteen stalls and four tack rooms. There were also two bathrooms and a kitchen with a refrigerator, microwave, and tables and chairs. There was a feed room, and when Poppy stuck her head in, the smell of fresh hay assaulted her. The scent made her homesick. Tammy introduced her to some of her horse tenants and gave Poppy a few treats to hand out before showing her the empty stall that Peggy would move into. Poppy was impressed. Not only did the floor contain a large amount of fresh shavings, but the feeder was state-of-the-art with safety features, and the automatic waterer was stainless steel. She had never seen anything like it. Her

Palamino could get used to this setup in a heartbeat. They left the barn by the rear entrance that led to the walker and the corrals. On the outside of the barn were two bays that could be used for a horse bath or horseshoeing. The corrals were large enough to give the horses plenty of room to exercise, and some bleacher seats were set up. She was taking all this in when she heard the clip-clop of horse hooves. Before she could turn around, she heard Tammy speak.

"Oh, here's my brother now. Poppy and Elizabeth, I'd like to introduce you to Kurt. He's the other half of the operation."

Kurt O'Shea sat tall in the saddle, which wasn't surprising for someone who, when standing, was six feet two inches tall. He and his sister, Tammy, both had blonde hair and brown eyes, but the similarities stopped there. Not that Tammy was unattractive—she wasn't. But she was a moderately attractive woman. Dressed as she was now, she fit the description of a 'plain Jane'. On the other hand, Kurt looked like he stepped out of a GQ magazine. Yes, he, too, dressed like a rancher, but on him, it only furthered his appeal. He could undoubtedly draw the ladies' attention with his big, toothy smile and warm personality. He had lived on the O'Shea Ranch most of his life with few exceptions. After high school, he attended LSU and majored in agriculture, but he realized after graduation that he wasn't quite ready to settle down. He had done some bronc riding and competitive calf roping when he was in high school and was quite good at it. He had the trophies to prove it. Kurt decided to give it a go and joined the Cajun

Rodeo Association. He would admit that he was a bit impulsive back then. He had just joined the Professional Rodeo Cowboys Association when he received the news that his father had died from a hemorrhagic stroke he suffered while out running some cattle. Of course, Kurt returned home. His mother had passed a few years before his dad. Tammy couldn't run the ranch alone, so Kurt retired from rodeoing and settled in. The truth was that he missed the farm life, and being on the rodeo circuit for two years was a lonely existence. He was pretty settled in here, working with the cattle and the horses. He and his sister inherited the ranch along with a large home that accommodated them easily as they each had their own wing of the house. He was comfortable living this life—for now.

    Poppy and Elizabeth turned around at the same time to say hello and recognized the cowboy from Pearl Creek! There was no way that Tammy missed the change in their expressions. Both of their faces were as red as a radish! She looked over at Kurt, who was grinning from ear to ear.
    "Okay, Kurt, can you tell me what is happening here? Do you already know Poppy and Elizabeth?" Tammy asked.
    "Let's just say we met…unconventionally at Pearl Creek when I was out looking for strays," Kurt said smiling.
    Poppy was so embarrassed she was temporarily at a loss for words. Elizabeth wasn't doing much better.
    "Poppy needed a place to board her horse, and her cousin recommended our ranch. Since we have accommodations, I offered her a stall for her mare. I was

showing her and her cousin around the property." But no one was listening to her speak. She knew there was something between the three of them that she wasn't privy to. But damned if she knew what it was. "Okay, you guys, what's going on here? How did you three meet?" Tammy asked.

Kurt looked at Poppy with a mischievous grin. "Do you want to enlighten my sister about our previous encounter?"

"No, you go ahead and tell her. I can see you're bursting with excitement," Poppy said.

"Well, the other day, when I was looking for strays down by Pearl Creek, I stumbled upon something I wasn't expecting. These two lovely ladies were skinny dipping," Kurt said, almost unable to contain his laughter.

"I sure hope Kurt was a gentleman. You know that water down there is crystal clear."

"We didn't find that out until he told us. We thought we were all alone until a cowboy rode up, sitting high on his horse. But he was a gentleman. Once he gave us the embarrassing news, he rode off. Elizabeth and I laughed about it later but never thought we'd run into him again," Poppy told Tammy. Then, looking at Kurt, she said, "Your sister told us those saddle bronc rider and roping trophies in the case belong to you. That's quite impressive. Were you ever afraid of falling?"

"No, I was never afraid of falling. I just hated hitting the ground," Kurt said with a laugh.

Tammy contained her laughter and immediately changed the subject. "You can give your transporter our address. Just let us know what day Peggy will arrive, and we'll take care of the rest." She couldn't suppress her laughter any longer, so out it came, and it was contagious.

Then Kurt looked from Poppy to Elizabeth, and they all laughed. What good is it if you can't laugh at yourself?

Poppy signed the papers for boarding and said goodbye to Kurt and Tammy O'Shea.

On their drive back to Leesville, all Poppy talked about was Kurt O'Shea. And all Elizabeth could think of was how Poppy could fall hard for this one.

CHAPTER 10

THE MOUNTED PATROL

Poppy couldn't miss the excited atmosphere as she walked into the Sheriff's Department. Several deputies were gathered around a large table and studying a map. Chief Deputy Tommy Jones looked up and studied her for a brief moment.

"Ms. Nichols, you wouldn't happen to have a horse, would you?" He asked.

"Yes, I do. I board her just west of Leesville. What's going on, Deputy?" She asked.

"We have a missing teenager in a two hundred thousand acre stretch of pine forest between Leesville and Burr Ferry.

We're calling out the troops. So, congratulations, you've just become a member of the Mounted Patrol!"

Poppy laughed. She could think of worse ways to spend an afternoon. And besides, she hoped she could help find the missing youth.

"We have a reserve deputy in charge of the unit, who'll be here in a few minutes. I want you to meet him, and he will fill you in on what to do," Tommy said.

Poppy had just settled back in her chair when her desk phone rang, and the receptionist advised her the head of the mounted patrol was up front. She hung up, walked to the front desk, and immediately did a double-take. Standing there was Kurt O'Shea. Upon seeing each other, they both had the same reaction.

"It's none other than the swimmer. I knew our paths would cross again. I didn't expect it to be so soon," Kurt said.

"You're in charge of the mounted patrol unit? I should have asked more questions before volunteering," Poppy said, laughing. "You seem to be everywhere, Kurt."

"You two know each other?" Tommy asked.

"We've met a couple of times. Once at my ranch where she boards her horse and the other time…" But Poppy was quick to interrupt Kurt.

"Take it easy, cowboy. Let's not go there," Poppy said, smiling.

They discussed their plan for the search and agreed that Poppy would meet Kurt at his ranch to pick up her horse. But, first, she had to return to the B&B, change into worn jeans and boots, and grab a hat.

When Poppy arrived at the ranch, Kurt had their horses trailered up and ready. It was only a ten-minute drive before they rendezvoused with the other deputies. Once mounted, Kurt asked Poppy to scan the brush as they rode but to stay close because of her unfamiliarity with the area. She readily agreed. They had ridden for an hour when she spotted what looked like a plaid pattern through the trees. She separated from Kurt to check it out. He started after her when he saw her ride away, planning to chastise her for the hasty departure. They both spotted him at the same time—the lost teenager. He was sitting on a stump with his head down and didn't hear them ride up. He looked lost and upset. They approached him at full gallop, and only when he heard the horses' hooves did he look up and holler to them while waving his arms. They dismounted and went to him, and immediately offered him some water. He was so glad to see another human being that he grabbed both simultaneously and hugged them as tightly as he could while tears streamed down his cheeks. He seemed to be okay, but Kurt checked him for injuries anyway. The boy was lucky because his only trauma appeared to be a few insect bites.

Poppy noticed that his look of relief quickly turned to fright. She wondered if there was something else going on here. Looking him square in the face, she asked, "Is there more you want to tell us?"

He nodded.

"Okay, spill it," Poppy said.

"I was out here with a girl. She slipped and hurt her ankle while we crossed the creek about a half mile back. It looked like she broke it. I was going for help when I got lost," he said.

Kurt looked at Poppy. "Okay, let's put him on the back of your horse and go find the girl."

Poppy didn't miss the look of anger on Kurt's face.

"It would be nice to know who we're looking for. What's the girl's name?" Kurt asked.

"Bella, Bella Jones," the boy answered.

"Are you kidding me? Are you talking about Judge Jones' granddaughter?" Kurt asked.

When the boy nodded, Kurt's look of anger became one of disgust. "Do her parents know that she's out here with you?"

The boy didn't answer; instead, he just shook his head.

Poppy didn't know the judge personally, but she had heard of his reputation as a stern, no-nonsense judge. She knew this wouldn't go down well and hoped they found the girl safe.

Twenty minutes later, they came riding up on Bella, sitting on the ground and leaning against a pine tree. She had her right knee bent and was holding her ankle. Kurt immediately got down off his horse and went to her. Bella recognized him immediately and looked relieved at the sight of him. He checked her ankle carefully and found it wasn't broken but badly sprained. He slowly picked her up and placed her in the saddle. Then Kurt climbed up on his horse behind Bella and gently held her on the ride back. Someone above had been looking out for them because either one could have been hurt even worse or bitten by a snake. They liked to curl up in the grass out here and strike anything that moves. Kurt immediately radioed the other units and advised them they had found the boy and a teenage girl who hadn't been reported missing. Thirty minutes later, the four of them had made their way back to the trailhead.

Poppy couldn't help but notice how Kurt handled the girl as he picked her up and put her on his horse. This was a serious side of him she hadn't seen before. Gone was his sarcasm—replaced with tenderness. She liked what she saw.

The boy's family was waiting at the trucks beside the road when Kurt, Poppy, and the teenagers emerged from the woods. They rushed over, the look of relief evident on their faces. Then they saw Bella Jones.

"Jimmy, you were supposed to be out here by yourself. What is Bella doing out here?" The boy's father asked.

Bella jumped in to defend Jimmy. "Mr. Lane, it was my fault. I knew Jimmy was going hiking, and I asked him if I could tag along. I doubt my parents even knew I was gone."

His parents were irritated at their son but very grateful he was found alive and without injury. They couldn't stop pumping Kurt and Poppy's hands and thanking them for finding the teenagers. Poppy didn't remember ever having her hand shook that hard. But it felt good being part of a team that had made a difference today. She liked the satisfaction that it gave her. Poppy and Kurt rode back to the horse trailer in silence. The adrenalin had wound down, but they both were still smiling.

Kurt was unloading the horses at the ranch when he turned to Poppy and asked her if she would like to have dinner with him that evening. Poppy looked at him quizzically because his invitation took her off guard. She hesitated, but only for a moment, before answering.

"Sure, Kurt, I would love to. Any particular reason?"

Kurt smiled and continued unloading the horses before answering her. "Well, if we need a reason, we can call it a celebration of a successful mission today. Those kids are lucky we found them unharmed. It could have turned out quite differently." As soon as the words were out of his mouth, he asked himself, 'Yes, Kurt, what is the reason for the invite?'. His next question to himself was, 'What am I getting myself into?'

CHAPTER 11

NICK DURANT

Stewart Lewis' cell phone rang, and a look at the caller ID told him it was Nick Durant. He'd been ignoring most of his calls of late. Especially since James died and Stewart had his suspicion that Durant was somehow involved. He knew Nick had a job for him, and like his brother before him, he wanted out of Nick Durant's business venture. If his father, Rufus Lewis, found out about his extracurricular work, he would be in a world of trouble, not to mention the conflict it would bring. With the McKays across the river, whom some suspected of killing James and Durant thirty-two miles down the river, whom Stewart was suspicious of, he knew that a battle with both simultaneously was unwinnable. He hesitated but knew he had to answer Nick eventually. He thought there was no time like the present and hit the speaker button.

"It's about time you answered the damn phone," Nick said, annoyed.

"What do you want, Nick?" Stewart asked unapologetically.

"Drop the attitude, Lewis. We have a meeting tonight at the office in Bon Wier. Make sure you're there. The boys have done well, and we have a mountain of products to move. Don't be late."

"Then you had better start without me because I'm out," Stewart said. He then ended the call.

Nick sat in his chair for a minute, stewing. No one dared to tell him *no*. There had to be a consequence for Stewart's insolence. It didn't matter that he was James' brother or that James was dead. If he let him off the hook, then others would try the same thing, and he would lose control. He didn't get where he was by running a loose operation. He needed to come up with a plan.

Nick decided to let Pete Seaux handle the situation and called him into the office. Without going into detail, he let Pete know that Stewart needed a tuning up, and Pete's orders were to persuade him to come back into the fold. Seaux was a small-framed man, but he made up for his lack of size in grit. He had been abused and pushed around as a kid and teenager. Finally, when he couldn't take any more, he got aggressive and developed a killer instinct. With the scars on his face and his beady dark eyes, he didn't need a calling card. His toughness was unmatched. Pete agreed to take care of this first thing tomorrow. Nick felt better about the situation because he knew that Pete would get Stewart under control. He also decided to offload his assignment for Stewart on someone else and would ask for a volunteer this time.

As Nick called the meeting to order, he went over old business before bringing up the new assignment. He let them know the latest haul was a big one. Marley Powell was the only one to volunteer. Durant felt that he was already losing control over these guys. Thankfully, Pete would handle Stewart Lewis quickly and send a powerful message to his rank and file.

Marley volunteered because he could see making a good side profit off the sales. Nothing like a bit of skimming. He'd done it before and hadn't been caught. And if he was, he certainly wasn't afraid of Nick or any of his idiots. So, what if he got caught? Just let them try something with him. He laughed as he thought of the rewards he would reap on the sale.

After the meeting, Nick asked Pete Seaux to hang back; he had another assignment for him. He wanted Pete to check all of Marley's sales and make sure he was reporting the correct purchase price of each sold item. He felt that Marley had been too eager to take on the sale of the property in question. Besides that, he had never trusted him and recognized him for the thief he was. Who else would be attracted to this kind of business?

Pete could be relied upon to complete any job Nick assigned him. So, it was no surprise that he was driving up to the Lewis home early the following day. After he pulled up to the front door, he sat in the car for a minute, looking around. Chickens were running loose, cattle were grazing in a pasture, and there sat some old, broken-down logging equipment that looked like they were cannibalizing it for parts. He sat back for a minute and laughed at this redneck haven. Thinking this would be easy, Seaux got out of his car ready to give Stewart Lewis an ultimatum. He was not even two feet from his car when the front door burst open, and a heavyset man with a beard stepped out with a .44 magnum pistol in his hand. Pete Seaux stopped dead in his tracks when he saw the gun.

"What you want, boy?" Rufus said with a growl.

"I'm here to see Stewart," Seaux snapped back.

"What's your business with him?" Rufus asked, getting angry. He already didn't like Seaux's attitude.

"That's between me and him. Is he home, old man?" Seaux said defiantly.

That's when Rufus lost it and put his hand on the magnum with his thumb on the hammer. "Boy, you have just enough time to get your ass back in that car and get off my property before you become fertilizer out in that field," he said while pointing to where his cattle were grazing.

Seaux stared at Rufus, who looked like a pissed-off grizzly bear. He could see Rufus' scowl under his thick, curly beard. Not only couldn't he be intimidated, but Seaux had no doubt he meant what he said and would follow it up with action. He wasted no time returning to his car. In fact, he dove into the driver's seat and had his speed at 45 MPH in about two seconds. As he was driving away, he looked in his rearview mirror and saw Rufus standing on the porch with pistol aimed, following him with his eyes. Pete Seaux's recommendation to Nick Durant was to find someone else to fence stolen property. Pete had no intention of returning to the Lewis homestead, ever!

CHAPTER 12

THE WARRANT

Elizabeth was sitting at her desk working on a report when she got an *IM* from Regional Headquarters in Shreveport advising her that she had an urgent encrypted email. She opened her mail and quickly read the message. A suspect had been identified in a rash of convenience store robberies in Louisiana and Texas. The suspect brandished a firearm in each case, but so far, he had not discharged it. Still, they considered him to be dangerous. His most recent address was in northwest Vernon Parish, where he lived with his brother. No agents were available in that office to assist her, so they advised Elizabeth to request help from the local sheriff. After reading the email, she contacted Sheriff Craft to ask for assistance from his office.

Without hesitation, he assigned Chief Deputy Tommy Jones and Deputies Jack Cooper and Doug Welch as backups.

Poppy was in her office when she couldn't help but see some deputies gearing up with bullet-proof vests and automatic weapons. Then she spotted Elizabeth walking in and doing the same. Getting up from her desk, she stepped into the hallway and asked Elizabeth what was happening.

"We have a federal warrant for a nasty dude up in the northwest part of the parish. Shreveport HQ has no backup available, so Sheriff Craft has lent me some of his deputies," Elizabeth told her.

Just then, Jerry Lambert came walking in and caught the last part of the conversation. He stood in the doorway, looking from Poppy to Elizabeth. "Are you talking about Marley Powell, who lives north of Hornbeck and the Sabine Parish line?" Jerry asked.

"That's the one," Elizabeth said.

Jerry advised them that the Powells were a dangerous bunch and that taking Marley wouldn't be easy. A couple of brothers and a half dozen cousins lived in that community, and they were no friends of law enforcement. He then announced that he was going with them because if you took on one of them, you took them all on.

"Okay, saddle up, amigo," Elizabeth said. She then looked at Poppy and asked, "Are you coming too?"

Poppy nodded, told her there was no way they were leaving her out of this caper, grabbed her Glock and five ammunition clips, and was out her office door.

"Poppy, follow Jerry into the tactical room and get suited up. That blouse you are wearing is very chic, but it won't stop a .223 round," Elizabeth advised.

It was still morning when the arrest team arrived at the Powell residence. The group stopped one hundred yards from the home and made a tactical observation. Elizabeth's plan was for the deputies to surround the house before she got on the bullhorn about fifty yards from the front door and announced they had a warrant for the arrest of Marley Powell. The deputies fanned out and went around to the rear and sides of the shack while Jerry and Poppy stayed with Elizabeth. When the perimeter of the residence was secure, Elizabeth picked up the bullhorn.

"Marley Powell, this is U.S. Deputy Marshall Elizabeth Weaver. I have a warrant for your arrest for robbery and interstate flight. Come out with your hands in the air, now!"

At first, there was nothing but silence. Just as Elizabeth was going to repeat her message, all hell broke loose. They were met with a volley of rounds from the house fired in their direction. Elizabeth immediately gave the order to return fire.

The dwelling wasn't much more than a termite-ridden shack with several windows covered with paper or cardboard.

An old truck was sitting on blocks to the left of the front door, and a beat-up sedan was behind the house. Once the shooting started, someone inside the house tore off the cardboard and returned fire with the arrest team. The occupants of the ramshackle dwelling didn't let up. They fired continuously, and the deputies fired right back as a furious gun battle ensued. As they fired, sections of the house were torn away. The team could hear yelling and cursing as the gunfire from both sides continued. This went on for what seemed to be an eternity but was more likely about ten minutes. Then, there was nothing but silence from the shack.

Elizabeth ordered her people to cease fire. She glanced at Jerry and Poppy, who were with her behind her car, and asked, "Are you guys okay?"

They both nodded their heads. She waited for the deputies to report in. When they did, they assured her that they had sustained no injuries. She looked at her car and noticed it hadn't fared as well as the deputies—it was full of bullet holes, but it could be replaced. Poppy looked at her gun and noticed she had gone through three clips and didn't remember reloading as she fired. She also didn't hear or feel the supersonic bullets that passed by her head on either side. Her heart wasn't pounding, and she didn't remember being scared, probably because she was too busy trying to hold the Powells at bay.

Elizabeth advised the team to move cautiously toward the house. When they entered, they saw three men lying on the floor. It was apparent they were all dead. The walls had not stopped the team's bullets. Their rounds tore through the house like it was a paper target. The Powells had been shot multiple times in all parts of their bodies, but they kept shooting back until their last breath. The team backed out of the house, and one of the deputies called the crime lab while Elizabeth called Sheriff Craft with an update.

When the crime lab arrived, they took over the scene. After fifteen minutes, the lab supervisor called Elizabeth over.
"See these three guys? None of them are Marley Powell. That one there," he said, pointing to a body by the coffee table, "is a cousin named Billy, and over there, the one lying dead in front of the couch is Marley's dad, Huey. The one by the wall is his twin brother, Harley. You can tell by the tattoo on his arm," he said. Sure enough, the guy was wearing a tank top, and you could see a tattoo of a 'chopper' with the word *Harley* stenciled under it. Elizabeth looked at the crime scene tech quizzically.
"I went to school with the Powells. I know them all, and I can tell you, they are an extremely dangerous family. Or they were."

Elizabeth and Poppy didn't know that Marley Powell was sitting on a hill half a mile away, watching as his family was taken out in body bags, one at a time. Seething with anger in his warped mind, he thought, someone is going to pay for this.

CHAPTER 13

THE ORCHESTRA

It had been several weeks since young James Lewis' body was found partially buried at the Sabine River. When the lab results came back shortly after, Sheriff Craft noted that there were signs of blunt force trauma to the left side of the boy's head. The deputies at the scene hadn't found anything in the boat or at the gravesite that would have been heavy enough to crush James' skull. Not much had happened since then, but that wasn't for lack of trying. There just hadn't been any solid leads. The case was getting cold. After talking with Sheriff Newman, he and Craft agreed that if Rufus Lewis didn't get some results real soon, he was going to get more than restless. He had said as much to Newman when they spoke a few days ago. And, if the Major thought Rufus was going to attack him, the Major would have his own plan already in place. Both Sheriffs knew that once the fighting started, it would be difficult to shut down, and people would die, so they spoke every few days to compare notes. Sheriff Craft was just ending one of those calls when Sheriff Newman asked Craft a question.

"Bobby, isn't there a man and his family that lives at the dead end of Trails End Road down in Evans? I'm pretty sure he's lived there most of his life. In fact, he's the third generation that has lived on the Sabine. No one would know the river like he does."

"I know him. That would be Jeff Simmons. Yeah, he doesn't cotton much to strangers, but he knows everything that happens on the Sabine. He harvests logs on the river, too, but neither Lewis nor McKay enter his section of the river. I don't know if that's because they have an unspoken agreement or because they are more afraid of him than of each other. It might be a good idea to send someone down there to talk to him, and I have a couple of people in mind," Craft said. Newman agreed with him.

When Sheriff Craft hung up, he walked down the hall to Poppy's office. She looked up as he walked in and took a seat.

"Poppy, I understand you have relatives in the Evans community, specifically the Simmons bunch."

"Yes, Sheriff, so my DNA test tells me, but I haven't met any of them yet," Poppy replied.

"Well, Poppy, today's the day you get to make their acquaintance. I would like you to interview a man named Jeff Simmons. His family has lived on the river for over one hundred years, and he has been down there most of his life. Not much happens there that he doesn't know about. Jeff knows every bend in the river—heck, you can't catch a fish without him knowing about it. Come to think of it, Elizabeth would be related to him, too. If she's available, I'd like the two of you to go speak to him. I'm guessing he's a pretty close relative. We need some development on the Lewis murder before things explode at the river."

"Sure, I'll go, and I'm sure Elizabeth will be willing to join me. But we're strangers to them. I don't expect they'll give us any special treatment."

"Poppy, one thing you will learn here in this part of Louisiana is that a blood relation carries a lot of weight whether they know you or not," Craft said with a smile.

Poppy hoped he was right and figured she'd find out soon enough. She wasted no time calling Elizabeth with his request; she was all in. There was no time like the present to introduce yourself to close kin.

They left the Sheriff's office in Poppy's truck, thinking they didn't want to ruffle any feathers down on the river with a marked unit. Elizabeth's replacement car had U.S. Deputy Marshall in large block letters on the side doors. Yeah, it was best they leave that vehicle behind, and the truck blended in better where they were going. The drive to the river took three-quarters of an hour, which neither of them minded. It was peaceful out this way—except for the occasional logging truck they passed on the road going in the opposite direction. Those trucks were large and intimidating.

"It's kind of early to visit someone, isn't it?" Poppy asked.

Elizabeth laughed at her question and the concerned look on her face. "These people down here on the river are early risers. By the time the sun comes up, they've been up for hours. Oh, by the way, Poppy, did you get moved into your rental house yesterday? If I didn't have to go to headquarters, I would have helped."

"Yes, I did. Kurt and a couple of his ranch hands took care of the heavy lifting. It's a cute little house with a white picket fence just west of town. Don't laugh, but it reminds me of a fairytale," Poppy said with a smile. "I was getting tired of the Bed and Breakfast. Don't get me wrong, they treated me nicely, and the food was good, but I was ready for more space and my own kitchen. You know, in case I want to entertain." She looked at Elizabeth with a grin on her face.

"Speaking of entertaining, you and Kurt seem to be spending a lot of time together lately." It was more a statement than a question. "Is that the type of entertaining you're talking about?"

Poppy didn't speak. She just smiled in response to her question.

Poppy was still apprehensive about meeting long-lost relatives and questioning them about a murder in the same conversation. When they arrived, they saw a three-story home beautifully landscaped with the river a hundred yards to the rear. As they got out of the car, two large hounds came out to greet them. Poppy could tell by their actions that all they wanted was a good scratch, so she accommodated them and patted them on the head. Elizabeth looked up and saw a man walking toward them from what looked to be a home-style sawmill. The man was tall and slim with long hair and a beard, in his late sixties, she would guess, dressed in overalls, a tee shirt, and a ball cap. He extended a tan, calloused hand when he got to their car.

"Good morning, ladies. I'm Jeff Simmons, and I own this little piece of paradise," his hands outstretched to indicate the house and the land that went with it. "What brings you to my part of the Sabine?"

"Well, Mr. Simmons, I'm U.S. Deputy Marshal Elizabeth Weaver, and this is Poppy Nichols with the Vernon Parish District Attorney's office. We're investigating the murder of James Lewis and are canvassing people up and down the river. I'm told that of all the people down here, we should talk to you first. It's said that you know anything worth knowing about the river. Would you have any information that you could share with us that would help our investigation?"

"Well, first things first," Jeff said with a smile, looking at Poppy.

"Your last name is Nichols? I went to school with Louis Nichols, who was a cousin. You any relation to him?" Jeff asked.

"Yes, he was my father. I never knew him. He and my mother died in a car accident when I was six months old."

"I'm sorry to hear that. He dated a girl throughout high school by the name of Abby James. I heard they had married, but I lost touch with Louis."

"Abby was my mother," Poppy said.

"Did you know Louis' sister?" Elizabeth asked.

"Sure, that was cousin Doris," Jeff replied.

"Doris is my mother. She and my father, Ben Weaver, live in the Dallas area. That's where I was raised," Elizabeth said.

"Well, it's a small world, isn't it? You girls are a nice surprise." Then Jeff turned and looked at Poppy. "I'm sorry you lost your parents, Poppy. They were good people. Well, I'm forgetting my manners. Come on in, sit, and have a cup of coffee. I'm happy to help, if possible, but I'm not sure how."

Once they were settled around the kitchen table with a cup of coffee, Poppy asked Jeff if he had seen anyone or anything suspicious on the river in the last few months. Anything out of the ordinary, she asked. He told them he knew almost everyone on the river. A few boats pass up and down, but very few stop. Jeff said there were hundreds of sinker logs out there, and he claimed all of them for a mile in each direction of his river property. According to him, since his family had cut the cypress trees on their property and floated them down the Sabine, the sinker logs in that section of the river belonged to him. He told Poppy and Elizabeth that he monitors anyone in that section or passing through because people try to poach his logs. But he said with a grin, they only try it once.

"Let's take a walk down to the Sabine, ladies, and let me show you around."

Jeff walked out the door and started walking toward the water. Elizabeth looked at Poppy and shrugged as if to say, 'I'm game if you are.' They both followed Jeff to a sandbar at the river's edge.

"See that old river?" Jeff asked, pointing in both directions. "My family has been on this section for one hundred and twenty years. I never get tired of that view or the Sabine River orchestra. All you have to do is remain silent for a moment and listen; you'll hear it," he said as he looked up and down the river. "I have walked into the Sabine a million times and never dipped my toes into the same waters twice. This old river changes every day yet remains the same. To me, this is my heaven on earth."

Poppy and Elizabeth stood still and totally silent. Then it hit them. That smell of the river and the perfume of the pine and cypress trees with a hint of magnolia in the air. The soft chirping of the birds, with the occasional caw of a hawk, lighted their senses as they watched and listened. They looked at Jeff, and for the first time, they heard what he heard and saw the beauty. The river had a rhythm. It played its own song. All you had to do was listen. After a few minutes, Jeff turned, looked at the girls, and motioned for them to follow him back to his house.

Jeff explained to them how things work on the river. He let them know that Rufus Lewis and the Major knew better than to enter his section of the river; they stayed clear. Pointing to the north, he told them McKay and Lewis' property was about three miles upriver. If you're looking for places to launch a boat, that would be at the old bait shack about a mile upriver run by a crusty 'River Rat' everyone calls Old Pat. His is the only place other than Lewis', McKay's, or my property. It's too swampy, or the bluffs are too high to get a boat on the water anywhere else.

Jeff told them he was sorry he couldn't be more helpful, but he was glad they had stopped by. He also told them that if they go by *Old Pat's Bait Shack*, they should tell Pat he had sent them. He mentioned that his wife Alice would be sorry she missed them—she was picking up some groceries in town. He asked them to be sure to come back another time, and Poppy said she would. It's always nice to meet kin you didn't know about. She and Elizabeth left feeling they had a very productive morning and hoped their luck continued at their next stop.

CHAPTER 14

RIVER RAT

Old Pat's Bait Shack was a ten-minute ride from the Simmons' property. The dirt road leading to the launch site was rough and muddy. Poppy and Elizabeth bounced around in the truck for a few minutes as they traveled on it before they saw the river. Poppy groaned, thinking her truck would need a good washing when they returned to town. There it was; the landing site was in front of them and sat right on the river's bend. The area had large, old oak trees with Spanish moss hanging off them. It reminded Elizabeth of a scene from an old horror movie. A few picnic tables and some old BBQ grills were sitting under the shade of the oaks. They pulled up to the bait shack, and as they exited the truck, they smelled the river first, then the swamp flowers and the vegetation. But another smell mercilessly hit them. It was the stench of fish guts. They looked at each other with a grimace on their faces before walking inside.

Looking around the store, they didn't see anyone. They did see six long shelves filled with sundry items, such as crackers, chips, canned meat, and motor oil. Elizabeth walked to the counter where an old cash register was resting and looked behind it. Nope, there was no one there either. Just as the girls turned to walk out, an older man about six feet tall with balding grayish-blond hair and blue eyes came in the door. He sure fit Jeff Simmons' description of a crusty old man.

"You ladies looking for some bait? I got a good choice of red wigglers, night crawlers, crickets, redtail shiners, and black spot shiners. Now, if you want stink bait, I have some of that too; it's right next to the canned meat," the man said.

Elizabeth and Poppy looked at each other and couldn't help laughing. The older man started laughing, too. He knew they weren't laughing at him but with him because they sure weren't going fishing by the way they were dressed.

"You must be Old Pat. I'm Elizabeth Weaver with the U.S. Marshall's Service, and this is Poppy Nichols with the Vernon Parish District Attorney's office. Jeff Simmons told us to look you up. We have some questions, and he thought maybe you could help us. But before we start, could I ask you what stink bait is?"

"Sure thing! But words won't do the trick. It's better explained by smelling it." Pat walked to the canned meat display, and, at the very end, he took a tin off the shelf. Walking back over to where the girls were standing, he opened the can and motioned for them to lean in and inhale. They each bent over and took a whiff.

"Good God, that just melted my brain. The taste is on the back of my tongue," Poppy said while gagging and spitting on the floor.

Elizabeth was trying to form a word, but nothing would come out. Finally, she got enough air where she could put a sentence together. Her eyes were crossed as she stuttered for a second or two and then spoke.

"I think that smell burnt the hairs in my nose. I can't smell anything but that damn bait. Is it possible to shampoo the inside of your nose?" Elizabeth asked.

Pat was leaning on the counter, laughing so hard he couldn't stand up straight.

"As soon as we get back to Leesville, I'm burning my clothes," Poppy said.

Pat handed each of them a soda, then put some coffee beans in a cup and told them to smell them for a minute.

"So, I guess you ladies didn't come all the way out here to smell stink bait. What can I do for you?" Old Pat asked, still laughing.

"Pat, can I ask you a question? It's about the stink bait," Elizabeth said.

Old Pat nodded.

"Can't you smell that?" Pointing to the can of stink bait.

"Yes, but not much. I haven't had a bath in a week, and I just finished a Limburger cheese and mustard sardine sandwich before you girls showed up. I couldn't smell a skunk if he were behind the cash register. That stink bait smells better than me or that damn sandwich," Old Pat said, continuing to laugh.

"Oh damn, gimme those beans," Poppy said, laughing. Then, she got down to business. "I suppose you have heard about the James Lewis murder? We're asking people on the river if they saw anything suspicious around the time he went missing. But what we want to know from you is if you saw anyone launch a boat in the past few months that looked like they weren't going fishing. That includes people you know and anyone you don't know," Poppy said as she took another whiff of the coffee beans.

Just then, Elizabeth reached out and grabbed the beans from Poppy.

"Well, sometimes I get guys coming in here that are after sinker logs. I warn them off by telling them that if they go south, Jeff Simmons will send them on their way, and not too politely either. If they go north, they will have to contend with either the Lewises or the McKays. They don't want to tangle with them. That usually turns them around. The rest are just fishing. Come to think about it, there was this guy, a big fellow who launched his boat here a bit ago. It didn't appear that he was going fishing cause he didn't have any bait or tackle with him, and I didn't see any equipment he could use to pull sinker logs out of the river. I didn't ask him what he was doing 'cause

I figured it was none of my business as long as he paid his launch fee."

"Can you remember anything else about his appearance besides that he was a big guy?" Poppy asked as she took the coffee beans from Elizabeth.

"Oh, sure, I made note of what he looked like because I hadn't seen him around before. At least I couldn't place him as being from around these parts. As I said, he was a large guy, white, over six feet tall, and I'm guessing he weighed over two hundred and fifty pounds. He was driving a white Chevy pickup with Texas tags. Besides paying the launch fee, he gave me ten dollars extra for launching the boat for him. He didn't have a motor, just a heavy-looking paddle. He was gone for about two hours, I'd say. When he came back, he loaded up his boat and left before I could come out and talk to him. I thought he might need help getting the boat out of the water, but he managed just fine. That's about all I know."

"Would you recognize him if you saw him again?" Elizabeth asked with her nose still in the coffee beans.

"I think so."

They wrote down all the information Old Pat could remember and then asked him to call if he saw the man again. Poppy thanked him and started to walk off, but Elizabeth turned and faced Old Pat with one more question.

"May I keep these coffee beans until I fully regain consciousness?" she asked with a smile.

Old Pat smiled back at her and nodded. "They're all yours. Do you maybe want to take some of that stink bait with you?" he asked with a grin.

They smiled and shook their heads as they walked to Poppy's truck.

As they shut the doors to drive off, Old Pat leaned against the bait shack's front door and yelled, "If you want to smell that stink bait again, remember it will be at the end of the shelf right next to the caviar."

Elizabeth leaned out the truck window and hollered back to Old Pat, "I'd rather kiss a mule's ass than smell that stink bait again!"

"Do you think there's any chance in hell that we are related to Old Pat?" Poppy asked, laughing.

"Probably, but I haven't craved the smell of stink bait, sardines, or Limburger cheese lately. Make that never!" Elizabeth said, with her nose stuck in the coffee beans.

CHAPTER 15

THE JOURNAL

Poppy had run into the Market Basket grocery store on Saturday morning to pick up a few delicacies for a small dinner she was planning that evening. Actually, it was a dinner for two—her and Kurt. She told herself it was to repay him for the dinner he had cooked for her, but it was a good excuse to spend more time with him. Kurt had suggested she pick up some boudin and promised he would teach her how to prepare it properly. When she came to Vernon Parish, it was for a job opportunity. She didn't know at the time if she would plant roots here. After all, her adoptive family was back in Georgia. Her cousins, Rory, Hannah, and Alex, were spread out over a few states, but they all returned to the fold for every major holiday. They wouldn't miss spending a Christmas with their mother, Charlotte MacHen. Poppy thought she would be homesick when she took this job, even though she had several blood relatives here. But she was settling in nicely, and Kurt was becoming a good friend to her. If she admitted the truth, she had begun to consider him more than a friend. She was starting to believe he felt the same way. She wasn't trying to rush a relationship—she was comfortable and happy with how things were going and enjoyed his company. She did miss her mother, Grace, however. From the age of thirteen until she graduated from law school, Grace had been her everything—her mother, father, cheerleader when she needed one, disciplinarian when required, and teacher of most things she would need in life.

She was lost in these thoughts when someone called her name. Looking up, she saw Jeff Simmons in the bread aisle. Standing beside him was an attractive woman with dark hair and a slight build.

After giving Poppy a big hug, he introduced her to the woman beside him. "This is my wife, Alice. When I told her about meeting you and Elizabeth the other day, she was disappointed she had missed you on that visit. That's why we decided to have a fish fry and BBQ a week from Sunday at our place on the river."

Just then, Alice interrupted him. "Well, it's one of the reasons we are having the BBQ. We do a family gathering occasionally, and I asked Jeff to contact you and Elizabeth. We had you in mind when we planned it. The relatives we invited are eager to meet Louis and Abby's daughter. But I wanted to make sure you could come before putting the final touches on the arrangements. Please tell me you're not busy. It will give you a chance to meet some of your Louisiana family," Alice said.

Before Poppy could answer, Jeff spoke up.

"When Alice says you will meet some of your family, we lean heavily on the word *some.* If we invited everyone in a thirty-mile radius that we're related to, we'd be cooking for a week!"

Alice rolled her eyes at him and laughed out loud. Poppy liked Alice immediately. She was so warm and friendly. If the others she met at the BBQ were this welcoming, she would be in for a good time. She decided to accept.

"I can't commit for Elizabeth, but I would be delighted to come. I'll give her a call as soon as I get home and pass on the invitation."

Jeff couldn't help teasing her a bit. "I hope you're still excited after meeting this branch of the family and pray their prying eyes don't scare you away."

"Hush now, Jeff, you're going to talk her into staying home!" Alice said.

"No, you won't do that. Since I arrived here, I've gotten used to people being curious about my heritage. Good thing I'm not a shrinking violet. By the way, is there anything that I can bring to the BBQ, a side dish or a dessert?" Poppy asked.

"No, you're our guest. Just bring yourself and Elizabeth. And make sure you dress casually. We'll be outside most of the time, soaking up nature," Alice told her.

"Will do. See you next Sunday," Poppy said, giving Alice and Jeff a big hug.

Poppy couldn't wait to complete her grocery list so she could go home and call her cousin. She hoped Elizabeth didn't have plans for the day of the BBQ. Running into Jeff and meeting Alice was a great diversion and one she probably needed. Thoughts of Kurt had gone straight out of her head. Poppy hoped she wasn't getting close to Kurt as a replacement for missing her mother. She thought what she felt for him was real, but based on what? She hadn't had that much experience with men—she hadn't had the time between school and work. She would just take it slow and easy and enjoy the ride!

Poppy called Elizabeth as soon as she got home to share the invitation to the BBQ with her. She told her about her conversation with their cousin Jeff and meeting his wife, Alice, at the market. "Please say you are free that day. If I'm going to be meeting a bunch of relatives, I could sure use some backup. Oh, and you will really like Alice. She's what I've heard people around here refer to as *good people*. Yes, that term fits her to a Tee! I could feel a genuine warmth when I spoke to her. Can you tell I'm excited about this BBQ?"

Elizabeth laughed. "Well, how can I say no with an introduction like that? Of course, I'll go with you. I've met some of my Louisiana relatives, but from what you're portraying, it sounds like I've only scratched the surface. It should be fun. And after your build-up about Alice, I can't wait to meet her."

"Great, let's plan to ride out there together. Oh, and I was at the market because I'm cooking a boudin dinner for Kurt tonight at his request. For me, that's an enormous risk. My cooking skills aren't all that great, and I've not only never cooked boudin, I've never eaten it! What was I thinking? Cooking for this man may ruin the relationship," Poppy said, laughing.

Elizabeth couldn't help teasing her cousin. "So, here's where the space for entertaining is coming in handy. Tell me, do you plan to entertain anyone besides Kurt?"

When Poppy awakened the following Sunday morning, she was surprised at how chilly it was. She looked at the temperature gauge just outside the front door; forty-five degrees, it read. She shivered as she walked out to the gate to retrieve the Sunday paper. This chill reminds me of being home in Georgia and realized it was a pleasant thought. She would have to dress appropriately for this weather and the outdoors today. Alice did say they would be outside. Jeans were a no-brainer, but what would she wear for a top? Mentally going through her wardrobe, she thought of the oversized yellow sweater that had been a gift from her mother. Wearing it would be apropos as it would remind her of her adoptive mother while she was meeting her blood relatives for the first time. The thought made her miss Grace, but she would be talking to her later that evening. She couldn't wait to tell her about the dinner she cooked for Kurt!

While Poppy drove, she shared with Elizabeth details of her evening with Kurt. Oh, but not all the details. Some things were worth savoring and keeping to yourself. At noon, they arrived at the Simmons' home. As Poppy got out of the truck, she recognized the scent of cedar in the breeze coming off the river. The smell of an oak and hickory fire was also in the air. The chill actually felt refreshing. Elizabeth closed the truck door, then looked around and saw a group of people. It looked like thirty or forty people gathered around a large barbecue pit and a pot of hot oil that sat on a burner.

"Poppy, do you think we are related to all these people?" Elizabeth asked with a laugh.

Before Poppy could answer, Alice was walking out to greet them.

"So glad you could make it Poppy. This must be Elizabeth. Both of you come on over here and meet some family," Alice said with a smile.

Elizabeth's question was quickly answered as they were introduced to one family member after another. It was exciting for Poppy because each of them had an anecdote to tell about either her mother or father. The stories they shared helped

Poppy paint a picture of them that she hadn't had before. She was so grateful to Jeff and Alice for putting this reunion together for her. As she stepped away from what she thought was a second cousin on her father's side, she was approached by Alice, who was walking with an older man. He wore a wide-brim black hat and had a warm and gentle look. Walking slightly bent over, he approached Poppy and Elizabeth. He looked up at the girls and smiled.

"Poppy, this is Uncle Wesley, your great uncle. He's eager to meet you," Alice said.

As he approached her side, Wesley reached out a callused, weathered hand and placed it in Poppy's. In his other hand, he held a small box with loose wrapping, as if the package had been opened, and then the wrap reattached. He smiled at the girls but focused his gaze on Poppy.

"So, you're Poppy," Wesley said with a smile.

"Yes, Sir, I sure am," Poppy replied.

"I have something I want to give you. It came to me three years ago. After opening it, I read it and then put it away. I didn't know where you were or if you even existed. It's been in my hall closet ever since. When I heard that fate had brought you here to Vernon Parish, I knew just what I needed to do with it." Then he handed the package to Poppy.

She took it from him while giving him a quizzical look. Hesitantly, she removed the wrapping and took the lid off the box. There, she found a letter lying on top of a journal. There was an address on the envelope that read:

Sheriff Donald O'Sullivan, Franklin County, Georgia.

Curiously, she opened the envelope and read the letter that was addressed to her Uncle Wesley.

Dear Sir,

This package was found this past week in a vehicle that had been wrecked some years ago and was sitting in a private junkyard. It was being stripped for parts when the mechanic saw this Journal lying in the trunk. The salvage yard owner called my department, and we placed it in our custody. We located your name under relatives listed on the last page. It wasn't difficult to look up your address. The book belonged to Abby Nichols. She mentions a daughter named Poppy in her writings, but we have no record of a Poppy Nichols. However, a review of our files shows that Abby and Louis Nichols, husband and wife, were killed in a truck accident twenty-four years ago. Per the report, a child was in the vehicle with them, but records from back then were lost, and there is no further mention of the child. If she survived, she would have been turned over to family services, but we have no way to verify that. If she is your relative, I sincerely hope you will be united with her one day. I hope these writings comfort you.

Warmest Regards
Sheriff Donald O'Sullivan

Poppy slowly lowered the hand that held the letter down to her side and looked up at Elizabeth. Then she turned her attention to Wesley.

"Thank you, Uncle Wesley, for this gift," Poppy said with glistening eyes.

"Aren't you going to read the journal?" Wesley asked.

"Yes, Sir, every single page of it. When I am in a place and time where it's quiet, and I can get a true feeling of my mother. I can't do that now. Besides, I would be too emotional. I can't tell you what this means to me," Poppy said in a low voice.

Wesley nodded. He understood what a shock it would be, reading what could be your mother's last words. He had gotten emotional when he read it three years ago. He was glad it was now in the right hands.

Poppy leaned over and kissed Uncle Wesley on his cheek, then headed towards her truck. She used her sleeve to wipe away the tears escaping from her eyes. She gently placed the journal on her front seat and touched it briefly. She could almost feel a heartbeat as her hand lay on the cover. She took a deep breath, wiped her eyes again, and then returned to the BBQ.

Poppy had regained her composure and had a smile on her face when she rejoined Uncle Wesley and Elizabeth. This day was certainly shaping up to be a good one. She scanned the crowd until she found Alice and walked over to her. "Are all these people my relatives?" She asked.

Alice laughed and responded, "Most. Except for that guy," she said as she pointed toward a man with dark hair and a short-cropped beard. "He's not related, but he's someone you should get to know in the Evans area." She gestured towards the man, "Sam, come over here for a minute."

Unable to refuse Alice anything, he walked over to where they were standing. He smiled as he approached and extended his hand.

"Poppy, this is Sam Haas. Sam is your man whenever you need information about anything happening on the Sabine River. Between him and Jeff, nothing goes unnoticed," Alice said.

"Pleased to meet you, Sam." She decided to put Sam's knowledge to work and switched gears, putting her Assistant District Attorney hat on. She advised him that she was one of several investigators who were working on the murder case of James Lewis, knowing he must have knowledge of the case. You couldn't know the Sabine River and not have heard of the gruesome discovery. So, she asked him if he had seen anyone or anything suspicious on the river during the time frame of James' murder.

Sam wasted no time in answering her. "Yes, that was a mournful day. I helped look for James' body along with several others. We all thought he had fallen out of the boat and drowned. Sad business, that was. Of course, it was sadder yet when Chad Perkins found his body. We're all neighbors out here on the river, and to think someone would do that to that boy? It's been really hard on his mamma and his father. Since that discovery, I've been wracking my brain, wondering if I'd seen anything out of place."

"And have you come up with anything?" Poppy asked.

"Well, there was something that didn't set right. I didn't think much of it at the time. I've lived out here my whole life and know almost everyone on the river. I'm not sure if it was the same day that James went missing, but I did see someone I didn't know. If it wasn't that day, it was close. I was on the river and saw a man with a large build paddling a boat up the river. It was unusual not to have a motor, but what caught my attention was that he was paddling against the current."

When he said that, Poppy leaned in towards him and asked, "What else do you remember about him?"

"I assumed he had launched from *Old Pat's Bait Shack*. I waved to him, and he looked at me. We were only twenty feet apart, but he didn't wave back. That's not custom for folks out here. They're usually pretty friendly."

"Would you recognize him again?" Poppy asked.

"Sure, no doubt. I got a good look at him. You know I could see into his boat. He had no fishing tackle...I mean nothing, just him and that large paddle. It was strange for someone to be on the river just paddling around."

"Thanks, Sam. You've been a big help. We had someone else give us a similar description. Sounds like we have a solid lead on a suspect," Poppy said out loud but thought to herself, 'If we only had a name.'

It had been a wonderful day. She had met more relatives than she could have ever imagined just a few short months ago. After meeting Uncle Wesley and receiving the journal, she couldn't keep her mind focused. Poppy would be talking to a newly found relative, and thoughts of that journal would creep into her head. She was curious about what was inside. What had her mother written that might be important to her or that might open another door? Well, she was about to find out. Even though it was late when she returned home, she took the journal off the front seat, held it close to her chest, and entered the house. She gently laid the book down on the coffee table. Its contents would have to wait a few minutes while she changed into a robe. With that done, she settled into the corner of the couch and was ready to read her mother's words. She picked up the book and started turning the pages. Her mother must have loved to write as the pages were crammed full of information. Some of her mother's thoughts warmed her heart, and some were shocking. As she turned the pages, Abby and Louis' life unfolded.

Louis Nichols asked me to go to the Freshman Dance today. I can't believe it. He is the best-looking boy at Evans High School. Of course, I said yes. I haven't told my parents yet. I'm waiting because I'm afraid they will say I'm too young to be dating. I'm already putting together arguments in my head to present as to why they should let me go. The first one I've thought of is that there will be chaperones there. What could possibly happen at a chaperoned dance? My next possibility is asking Louis to come over for Sunday dinner before the dance so they can meet him. I just know if they meet him, they will love him. Okay, love is a strong word, but they'll like him for sure.

Yes! My parents said yes! Louis put on his Sunday best and came to our house for dinner. He was such a perfect gentleman they couldn't resist him. He complimented Mom on her cooking and asked Dad about his new tractor. Well, not brand new, but new to him. It was an Allis-Chalmers, and it had power steering. According to Dad, it was unheard of before 1950. We hadn't even eaten the chocolate cream pie yet when I could see he had won them over. Louis and I were going to the Freshman Dance on an actual date.

Today, Louis asked me to go steady. I wasn't expecting it. But I was hoping he would. He gave me his high school ring, and I'm going to buy a chain so I can wear it around my neck. I might keep it under my blouse for the first few days while I'm home. I'm not sure what my parents will have to say about it. I can hear my mother now, 'Abby, it's just too soon. You've only been seeing the boy for a few weeks.' And, of course, I will tell her I've known him much longer than that! I won't tell her that I dreamed about him for eons before he asked me out. I plan to wear Louis' ring on the outside of my blouse, front and center, for everyone else to see though. I want to shout, 'I'm proud to be Louis Nichols' girlfriend!'

It's Friday night, and I sat in the bleachers at Evans tonight with my girlfriends and watched as Louis played point guard. The matchup was against Rosepine, a big basketball rival. Evans won, and Louis had done his share of setting up the plays. Afterward, he was being congratulated by so many students and parents alike that I couldn't get near him. But after the game came my turn. We sat in his truck and talked and kissed.

Poppy was getting tired, but she wanted to read the entire journal. She decided to fast forward to Senior year and save the rest for later. That way, she could 'fill in the blanks'. She was anxious to read about them in their married years— the few they had together. She was too excited and couldn't sleep until she found out more.

Wow, what a great night. There's no other way to explain it. We got home a little bit late, but my parents were still up. We went to the Burr Ferry Catfish House. All our friends were there, and we had milkshakes and cut-up. I always knew I was in love with Louis, and there was no one else for me. Tonight, he told me he felt the same. I don't think I'll be able to sleep!

I can't believe it; graduation is already happening. Louis and I have been going steady for four years, but he has been acting a little strange lately. I don't know if it's good or bad. I know he still cares for me. Lord, I couldn't stand it if he didn't. No, I think the future is on his mind. Once you graduate, you're pretty much an adult and have decisions to make. I sure hope that's all it is.

We just returned from the Leesville Steakhouse, and guess what? Louis asked me to marry him, and I said yes! Of course, I'll go to college first. I've worked too hard to pass it up. And besides that, my parents would never forgive me. They want better for me than they had. Dad has never been ashamed of being a farmer. He always says, 'It's the farmers of this country that feed the hordes.'

Poppy couldn't believe it. Her parents were engaged right out of high school. That wasn't something she could identify with. She couldn't think of a single boy that she went to school with that she would have wanted to spend the rest of her life with. I guess when you know, you know. Poppy skipped several pages but marked them with a paper clip to read later. She found the entry where Abby talked about getting married.

It's May, and Louis and I are getting married tonight. It might sound corny to someone else, but I've always wanted a May wedding. But this won't be the wedding that I dreamed of. It's been three years since we graduated, and we've been together for seven years now. We thought we had waited long enough. After all, my grandparents married young and started having kids right away. Mom's argument is that was how it was done back then. Farmers needed help on the farm, and children did their fair share. There are many reasons my parents and Louis' parents say we shouldn't get married—just yet. Louis' parents say we are too young and my parents want me to finish college. But the truth is that Louis was offered a great job opportunity with a welding company in Georgia, and we don't want to be separated. We want to move there and start a new life as husband and wife.

Louis and I are married. This should have been the happiest day of my life, but my mom, dad, and Louis' parents were not there. That's because we didn't tell them. We didn't want to be talked out of it, and we didn't want to deal with the drama. We decided we would call them from Mississippi as we honeymoon across the south.

My journal was somehow misplaced on the move to Georgia. Thankfully, I found it in a box marked winter sweaters. I feel as if I found a long-lost friend. It's been a year since we've been back home to Evans, but today, we returned for a visit. We have some good news to share. Our family will increase by one in about six months. Louis and I are going to be parents to a little girl. I know I was made for this; I'm so happy and hope our parents are too.

My hopes of a happy reunion with our parents were dashed. The opinion they voiced was the same as when we told them we wanted to marry—they felt we were too young to start a family. I wanted my mother and father to be happy for us because it wasn't as if we told them we were planning a family. We told them we had a child on the way. There's a big difference. Our parents made their displeasure known, which spoiled our homecoming and our news. But the biggest spoiler came a few days before we were scheduled to return to Georgia.

Mother answered the phone and told Louis he had a phone call from a woman, then handed him the phone. We left the room to give him some privacy. I was thinking it might be the scheduler at his work. He had asked for time off during their busy season. When Louis hung up, he called out for me, saying he had to talk to me. One look at his ashen face told me it was something serious. In a faltering voice, Louis told me he had kept a secret from me. He had been ashamed of his actions then and didn't want me to be ashamed of him, too. While I was attending college, he'd had a brief affair with a woman who was engaged at the time to another man. To his chagrin, she told Louis she loved him and wanted to marry him, not her fiancé. Louis told her he was, in fact, engaged to another woman who he loved dearly. His actions were those of a lonely man missing his fiancé, and he advised her to follow through with her engagement and marriage to the other guy. Although she pleaded with him, he asked her not to call him again. He felt like a heal but hadn't heard from her until today when she told him she had a child and he was the father. Today, she explained that she had married the fiancé shortly after that, and her new husband believed he was the child's father. I forgave him, but that wasn't the end of it. Before we left Leesville, I saw the woman at the grocery store in Leesville. Or rather, she saw me. I didn't know who she was until she walked up to me and told me that she had a son who was a year and a half old, and it was Louis's child. What did she expect me to say? I stood there dumbfounded before I told her that I was having a daughter in six months. I left the store without purchasing a thing. I can't leave this place fast enough.

    Poppy paused for a moment. Did I just read that I have a half-brother? And who is his mother? Is she still married to the same man, and are they raising him as their son? Does the boy know about his birth father or for that fact about me? Probably not, or he would have sought me out. Or would he? I never expected this when I started reading this journal. It's too bad my father didn't have a journal; then, I would have had help figuring this out. Should I tell Elizabeth or forget about it? Of course, I'll tell Mom when we have our weekly update call on Sunday. Surely, everyone knows I have moved to Leesville, so if he knew about me and was curious, he could find me. And, if his mother still lives here, she would know who I am. There certainly are no secrets in Vernon Parish. I'm betting the son doesn't know. If I start asking questions, it would probably cause turmoil in that family or possibly destroy it. No, it's best to leave it alone. I'll tell Elizabeth, but that's as far as I'll take it.

She continued reading and hoped there were no other shocking revelations.

Today, our precious little girl came into the world. We decided to call her Poppy, like the flower. Although we immediately let both sets of grandparents know of her arrival, we didn't get a response from any of them. That's alright—we have our beautiful daughter to fill the void. And that she did.

It's been six months since Poppy arrived. I've been so busy with motherhood that I haven't had time to update my journal. Louis was promoted at work this week. He's now the new foreman. Things are looking good for our little family. We still haven't had any contact with our parents. We had thought that they would come around once our little girl was born, even though they made it clear on our visit to Leesville that they were not pleased with our decisions. But I couldn't forgive them because rejecting us meant they were rejecting our daughter, who was an innocent in this. I suppose we will contact them in a year or so; maybe send some baby pictures. At least, I can say we tried.

Poppy and I went to the pediatrician yesterday. He said that she was going to be tall and was a healthy baby. I was so happy; it showed that I was doing something right even without a mother to guide me on the 'ins and outs' of raising a child. When Louis gets home, we are going to the market to buy a bottle of wine and some steaks to celebrate his promotion.

Poppy looked at the date and turned a page. It was her mother's last entry. Did they die on the way to the market, she thought? Why didn't the people in authority try harder to find relatives? Maybe in the long game, it worked out for the best. Just think she could have been raised by grandparents who didn't want her. Poppy shut her eyes and took a deep breath. She now knew that she was the world to her parents. Her mother made it clear how much she was loved. Her next thought was that they sure didn't come any better than Grace MacDonald. Grace's love for her had taken the sting out of being parentless. But she couldn't forget that she had a brother somewhere, around twenty-seven or twenty-eight years old. She wondered if he was still in Vernon Parish and wanted to find him. But she knew it was probably best to leave things as they were. There was perhaps a good reason this secret had stayed buried for all these years, and she would have to leave it at that. For now, anyway. But could she?

CHAPTER 16

DOUBLE DATE

Poppy and Elizabeth were enjoying dinner with their respective dates. It had become a double date after Elizabeth invited herself and Jerry along. Poppy and Kurt O'Shea didn't mind the company; in fact, they decided to extend the dinner into an evening of fun. By unanimous agreement, they agreed to go to *The Oasis Club, one* of the many country venues in Leesville that played live music. The Cajun Cowboys, a local band, entertained them. So much so that they decided to get up and dance—after drinking a couple of glasses of wine. There's nothing like a bit of alcohol to liberate you! But the night was just getting started. When the band returned from a short break, they asked if anyone in the audience would like to sing with the band. Before Elizabeth knew what was happening, Jerry raised his hand and pointed a finger at her. She looked at him as if he were crazy. But then the groundswell of clapping and calls for her to take the stage grew louder. The crowd started chanting, 'Go, go, go.' Looking at Poppy, Elizabeth said, "They don't even know if I can sing."

Poppy encouraged her by saying it didn't matter if she could sing—no one would care because most of them were probably drunk anyway. It wasn't exactly positive reinforcement. Elizabeth was now regretting that they had come here. Whose idea was this? She didn't want to make a fool of herself but reluctantly made her way to the stage, wishing she had drunk a couple more glasses of wine. She leaned over and whispered something into the band leader's ear. He handed her his guitar, and she pulled her long blond hair back before putting the strap over her shoulder. Then she turned to the rest of the band and told them the key of G. She started playing the acoustic guitar, then the fiddle kicked in, then the drums. After one musical bar was played, the entire band started up. Elizabeth opened her mouth, and the words to *All American Girl* by Carrie Underwood poured out.

> *"And now, he's wrapped around her finger.*
> *She's the center of his world."*

When Elizabeth started hitting the high notes, the crowd started going wild, and the band members looked at each other and smiled with approval. The bass player looked at the lead guitar player and mouthed 'OMG'.

"And his heart belongs to that sweet, little, beautiful, wonderful, perfect All-American Girl."

As Elizabeth sang, she looked at Jerry, and he smiled back at her. If Jerry wasn't in love with Elizabeth before she sang, he was now.
Poppy turned and looked at Kurt, "She's singing to Jerry."
"I know. It's beautiful, isn't it?" Kurt said.

When Elizabeth finished the song and took the guitar strap off her shoulder, the bar patrons were on their feet, clapping, shouting, and whistling. She looked around in total amazement. The band laid their Instruments down and started clapping, too. Elizabeth looked back at the drummer, and he gave her two thumbs up. She couldn't believe what she was seeing. The response to her performance was overwhelming. Either she was that good, or they had over-imbibed. She walked back to the table, and Jerry stood up and kissed her before she could sit down. The crowd was still on its feet, but Jerry Lambert was the only one she wanted to impress.

Kurt looked over at Poppy, put his hand on her shoulder, bent over, and asked her if she knew how to sing. Poppy laughed and told him no. He leaned in, kissed her, pulled back for a second, and then looked at her with smoldering eyes. She thought she would melt. He tried to speak but found himself stuttering. When he finally found the words, they were, "Poppy

Nichols, I'm beginning to like you a lot; you're beginning to grow on me. I'm unsure what I'm feeling because I've never felt this way." Kurt immediately found himself embarrassed at what he had blurted out. Then compounded it with "I'm not doing this very well, am I?"

Poppy responded without hesitation and kissed him. "Keep going. You're doing just fine!"

CHAPTER 17

POACHING

The fog was beginning to lift off the Sabine River when Rufus Lewis and two of his sons stepped off the wide sand bar and got into a large, flat-bottomed riverboat. Rufus told his son Conor, who was operating the boat, to head north to the bend in the river and steer to the Louisiana side. He was going to get some sinker logs embedded in the sand and clay bank, even though, technically, they were on the Major's property. Rufus had a theory about how they had gotten there, but he hadn't argued his theory—yet. He would try it this way first. This was about more than who had the right to the sinker logs and more to do with punishing James' killer. He'd waited long enough for the Sheriff to name a suspect, but Rufus had his thoughts on 'who done it.' He couldn't prove it. If he could, he would have already settled the matter. Rufus decided to handle it differently. Knowing that the Major would find the sinker logs missing, he would know where to look and would come for them. Rufus smiled at the thought. As soon as the Major stepped foot on his property, Rufus would put a permanent end to their feud.

"Hey, Pop. This is on the Major's property," Conor said as he slowed the boat down.

"You never cease to amaze me, boy, with your brilliance," Rufus said in a deep, gravelly voice.

"Of course, it's the Major's property."

Conor eased the boat up to a large log that was partially embedded in the river bank. Rufus tied off the boat so the river's current wouldn't work against them. Tanner was wrapping a cable around the end of a log to be winched out of the bank. Suddenly, the silence was broken by the sound of a rifle round echoing off the river's bank and out over the water. The unexpected boom made the Lewises jump with fright. Tanner fell backward in the boat but was uninjured. He was just shaken and void of speech. Rufus looked over and saw a sizeable chunk had come flying off of the log that Tanner had put the cable around. He immediately pulled out his .44 magnum pistol and started looking toward the southeast, where he thought the round came from. The sun was rising, so Rufus had to squint his eyes to see in that direction. All was quiet for a minute. The Lewises looked for the shooter but could only see the last bit of fog gently rising off the water. Thinking the shooter had *hit and run*, they relaxed and sat down in the boat. Before their fannies hit the seats, a voice came from the woods high up on the bank of the river.

"Unhook that cable, Rufus," said the vaguely familiar voice.

Rufus was shocked but had no plans to show it. "Reveal yourself, coward!" he yelled.

The voice came back even louder this time. "You have one minute to take the cable off that log. I would make haste if I were you because I have my crosshairs on that boy in the front of the boat."

"Is that you, Major? Have you come to kill another of my boys?" Rufus asked.

"Thirty seconds left, Rufus. You'd better move it," the voice said.

Rufus yelled to Tanner, "Get that cable off the log, now!" Then, shouted to the voice in the woods. "This isn't the end of it. There will be another time!"

"There better not be, Rufus. Because the next time, I won't be so forgiving." The voice answered back.

The man's voice echoing off the riverbank walls, and the murky Sabine River sounded familiar. But damn if he could identify it as belonging to the Major. He thought it sure sounded like a McKay. Could it be one of the Major's sons or someone who worked for him? One thing he was sure of is that whoever it was knew him, and that was all that mattered.

Another shot rang out with a bullet round striking the front of the boat as a warning. Rufus holstered his pistol and told Conor to get them the hell out of there.

When Rufus returned home, he wasn't just mad; he was furious. He moored his boat at the sandbar, then took a look at the bullet hole in front. It was big enough to push a golf ball through. He was now certain that whoever was shooting wouldn't hesitate to put a bullet hole in him. Just let them come over to this side of the river. Rufus believed in tit for tat, and his gun wouldn't be aimed at a boat! His family had always had strong ties to the river, but it seemed the river had turned against him. His youngest son had been found dead—buried on the riverbank, and now those damn sinker logs had wedged themselves on the wrong side of the damn river! He felt helpless, which was not his nature. Even that damn Sheriff had been no help. Well, dadgummit, he had been hired to represent everyone in this county. Rufus picked up the phone and called the Cypress County Sheriff's Department. When the desk officer answered the phone, he asked for the Sheriff.

Sheriff Mitchell Newman was born in East Texas sixty years ago. He cast an impressive shadow at six feet tall and with his lean physique. He was first elected Sheriff of Cypress County twenty-five years ago and had run unopposed in every election but one—and he *smoked* that opponent. He was known as a no-nonsense type of guy—one that let you tell your story before putting you in jail. Newman wasn't much of a talker; he mostly listened. Texas law enforcement had a saying, *"One Riot, One Texas Ranger,"* meaning one is enough. East Texas had its own saying, *"I'll Call Sheriff Mitchell Newman."* He didn't need to show up, mind you. Just the threat of his appearance was enough to calm down a fracas or get a suspect to cooperate. Candidates for deputy had to pass his inspection before making it to the interview process. And even then, he hand-picked his deputies. Only professional lawmen need apply!

"Mitchell, this is Rufus Lewis. I was out on the Sabine early this morning with two of my sons when we were threatened and shot at twice. I want you to do your job and find out who was gunning for us!"

"What part of the river were you on, Rufus, when you were shot at?" Newman asked.

"Why should that matter? Look, someone is after me and my family, and I want something done, or the Sabine River will run red with blood!" Rufus growled.

"Rufus, you know which side matters. Now, exactly where were you?" The Sheriff asked.

"I was on the Louisiana side, Mitchell."

"And whose property were you on when you say someone shot at you?"

"Major McKay's property, but that doesn't give him the right to shoot at me and my boys," Rufus answered.

"Rufus, a few minutes ago, you said someone shot at you. Now, you're saying it was Major McKay. Did you see him? Do you have proof?" Mitchell asked.

"No, Mitchell, I didn't see him. Because if I had, I would have shot back at him! I didn't have to see 'somebody' to know the voice was that of a McKay. They all sound alike," Rufus answered.

"Look, Rufus, you are an intelligent man, and you know as well as anyone that I have no jurisdiction in another state. Just what were you doing on the McKay's property? Were you poaching logs?" The Sheriff asked.

There was silence on the other end of the phone line, so Sheriff Mitchell Newman assumed he was right. "Did you wake up this morning deciding to become a complete idiot? What would you like me to do—call Sheriff Craft in Vernon Parish, Louisiana, for you?"

"I didn't say I was poaching logs," Rufus said.

"Then what were you doing on that side of the river?" Newman asked.

Rufus finally answered. "Okay, I was going to take a few logs. But is that a reason to threaten and shoot at me and my boys?"

"You don't need me to answer that question for you, Rufus. You already know the answer." Then Sheriff Newman advised him to call his office if anything happened on the Texas side of the river. But until then, he needed to file a complaint with Sheriff Craft, or he could contact the U.S. Marshall Service in Vernon Parish. Other than that, he told him, "I can't help you." Then he hung up the phone.

This conversation did not sit well with Rufus Lewis. He was used to pushing people around until he got his way. Intimidation was his style, but he should have known that approach didn't work with Sheriff Newman. Apparently, it was also the style of the person shooting at him and his boys on the river today. He took Sheriff Newman's advice and called Sheriff Bobby Craft to file a report of the incident. But that wasn't the end. It might be time for him to take matters into his own hands. Hands that were capable of getting the job done.

CHAPTER 18

INCIDENT ON TEXAS HIGHWAY

Evan McKay's wife, Sophie, and their two-year-old daughter were returning home from an appointment with the pediatrician in Leesville when Conor and Tanner Lewis spotted her driving towards them on the Texas Highway. The boys decided to give her a bit of a scare. Once they came even with her on the road, they turned their truck around and started chasing her. As they got up near her, Conor, who was driving, came just inches from her bumper, causing her to swerve and almost leave the roadway. Terrified, she got on her phone and called her husband to tell him what was happening. Evan wasted no time jumping in his truck and picking up his brother Cody on the way to his wife's location. When the McKay brothers arrived, they saw that the Lewis boys were still closely following Sophie and teasing her rear bumper with the front of their truck. Seeing this, Evan became furious and realized this was more than a harmless game they were playing.

As Evan approached the Lewis truck, he swerved in front of it, causing Conor to lose control and land in the ditch. Sophie pulled over next to Evan on the highway, but he wasted few words advising her to go right home. He and Cody were going to take care of business. Sophie followed his instructions, pulled out on the highway, and headed home.

As the McKay brothers approached Conor and Tanner's truck, they could see the boys were still stunned by their unceremonious ditch landing. Evan and Cody opened the cab doors and pulled them out forcefully. Without saying a word, the McKays put a pretty bad beating on the Lewis boys. Evan was sure he had broken Conor's jaw and probably his nose. Cody hit Tanner multiple times in the face, causing large lacerations. It was going to be difficult for their mamma to recognize them. Both of the Lewises were bleeding profusely. The McKay brothers tied the Lewises up and threw them in the back of their pickup. Before leaving, they slashed all the tires on Conor Lewis' truck. Knowing Rufus Lewis pretty well, the McKay brothers knew he wouldn't take the beating of his boys lightly. They knew to be prepared, so they made a special delivery right to his doorstep.

Evan stopped the truck twenty feet from the house's front door, then leaned on the horn. He and Cody got out, walked to the rear, pulled the Lewis boys from the truck bed, and rolled them onto the ground. Rufus Lewis opened the screen door, came out, and stood on the large porch to see what the commotion was all about. As he stood there, he observed his two boys being tossed on the ground like trussed-up hogs. He looked at Conor and Tanner's faces and saw they were covered with blood and dirt. He was a big man about to go berserk. He could tell they had been severely beaten as he stood there staring at his sons lying on the ground. As the breeze off the river covered the boys with another layer of dirt, his sons looked up at him. They couldn't move because of the bindings and couldn't speak because one of them had a broken jaw, and the other had a thick coat of blood covering his face, with his mouth so full of dirt he couldn't spit out.

He looked at the McKay boys and asked them in a deep, angry voice why they had done this to his sons. Evan relayed the events of what happened on the Texas Highway to him, leaving out no details.

"It was your idiot sons that assaulted my wife and baby girl on the Texas Highway and tried to run them off the road. They could have been killed," Evan said, staring at Rufus angrily.

Evan continued to tell him that his sons were cowards and lowlifes and had the manners of swamp trash. They wanted to terrorize women and children instead of fighting grown men. He proceeded to tell Rufus that if he ever caught those two stinking river rats on the Louisiana side of the river again, he would kill them both.

As Evan turned to leave, Rufus told him and Cody to hold on. "I understand why you're upset, but to beat my sons this severely isn't forgivable." He then put his hand on his .44 Magnum pistol.

"Before you pull that pistol, Rufus, I suggest you look at my brother Cody," Evan said, nodding toward his brother.

Rufus looked in Cody's direction and realized he had a sawed-off 12-gauge shotgun pointed right at his ample midsection.

"Don't test me, Rufus. All I need is a reason. I won't hesitate to cut you right in half," Cody told him.

Rufus' wife heard the commotion, saw the boys on the ground, and saw Rufus put his hand on his pistol. She dropped the dish she was drying and came running through the door to the front porch. She looked at the McKay boys and saw the shotgun in Cody's hands.

"Please don't kill him," she screamed. "We have already lost a son. I can't lose my husband."

"Get back in the house, woman!" Rufus demanded.

But she refused to leave and moved closer to him with her head down.

Rufus looked at Cody and took his hand off the pistol to end the stand-off. He saw the hate in Cody's eyes and knew he would be a dead man if he didn't holster his weapon. Taking a long, hard look at the McKays, he told them to get off of his property and that if they ever came back, there would be bloodshed on both sides.

Evan nodded but had one more piece of information for Rufus to contemplate before he left. "If you want the boys' truck back, it's about five miles east of the river bridge on the Texas Highway. I suggest you bring something to tow it with because it's not going anywhere on its own steam."

Rufus watched them leave before turning to address his boys. He was so mad you could see the red in his face illuminating through his thick beard.

"You two don't have the sense that God gave a sloth. What made you idiots go after a woman and a child? Better yet, how in the hell did you let two McKay boys beat you down like a dog? If you weren't already in such bad shape, I would put a beating on you myself. You two fools aren't going anywhere or doing anything unless you have my permission." Then he cut the restraints from Conor and Tanner's arms and legs.

"Stewart! Get out here!" Rufus yelled. "Take these two idiots to the emergency room in Jasper."

"Leesville is a lot closer, Papa," Stewart said.

"Did all of the boys I raised turn out to be idiots?" Rufus asked in an angry, low growl. "Did you happen to hear what the McKays said? We don't need any more Lewis bloodshed. Take 'em to Jasper, like I said, fool. I don't want you setting foot in Louisiana."

Rufus looked over at Conor. "And you? You're supposed to be the tough one. And you took a whipping like that?" Knowing full well that Conor couldn't answer him. Rufus looked at him and said, "Hopefully, the doctors in Jasper can put your face back together.

After leaving the Lewis property, Evan and Cody went directly to their father's house. The Major had already heard from Sophie what had happened to her on the road. He was fuming mad at Rufus' boys for what they put not only Evan's wife through but also their little girl. The Major was known as a pretty tough guy, but he sure had a soft spot for his grandchildren. The boys proceeded to tell the Major what happened on the Texas Highway after Sophie had left. He didn't need to ask how Rufus reacted; he knew. The only question was, how would Rufus retaliate? Because the Major knew he would. After discussing the incident with Margo, she insisted that they call Sheriff Craft just so there would be a record of what transpired. A correct record because who knew what story the Lewis boys would tell?

After collecting his thoughts, the Major decided to call Sheriff Craft to ask him if any accidents had been reported out on the Texas Highway that afternoon. He told the Sheriff that his daughter-in-law and granddaughter had witnessed someone in a truck driving at a high rate of speed and weaving in and out of traffic. He assured the Sheriff they were okay but hoped the highway menace hadn't caused an accident. The Sheriff, although he thought the call from the Major was odd, told him that, as a matter of fact, a pickup had been found crashed in a ditch. There were no occupants and no other vehicles involved. A local farmer had reported seeing the truck but hadn't witnessed how it had gotten into the ditch. They were running the tags now to see who it belonged to. They checked the Leesville Hospital, and no one had been admitted with injuries from a vehicle accident. He offered to send a deputy out to interview his daughter-in-law, but the Major assured him she couldn't add more than what he had already told him. He thanked the Sheriff and hung up, thinking that would be the end of the incident from a law enforcement point of view. This wasn't good news to the Major. In fact, it was a sure sign that Rufus Lewis planned on handling it himself.

Sherrif Craft's office had already run the tags and knew the truck belonged to the Lewis family. This phone call from the Major told him there was more to this. He couldn't ignore the bad blood between these families, especially in light of the death of James Lewis. He didn't want more killing on either side of the State line. He planned to investigate further.

The Vernon Parish Sheriff's Department contacted the U.S. Deputy Marshall Service with a request to investigate a traffic incident. The Commander in charge in Shreveport thought it was an odd request. Since when has the Marshall Service been asked to look into a traffic accident? The Sheriff started by explaining there was a multi-jurisdictional issue with some folks involved from Louisiana and some from Texas. He further explained that it might have a connection to a death once thought accidental but was now a homicide. The Commander agreed to contact the Marshall assigned to Vernon Parish and put her on the case.

Elizabeth wasn't surprised when she was assigned the task of looking into what appeared to be a traffic accident but could be much more. She'd already heard some chatter about it around the office. Following protocol, she contacted Tim O'Connor, the District Attorney, and asked if Poppy Nichols was available to work the case with her. She felt that two women, not in uniform, would make it easier for both parties to speak with them—especially the Lewises. The District Attorney and the Sheriff agreed with Elizabeth's assessment and allowed her to take Poppy with her.

"I know you haven't been here long enough to get your feet wet. Well, except for our excursion to Pearl Creek," Elizabeth said with a laugh.

Poppy smiled at her and asked, "What do you have in mind?"

"I'm about to jump into the deep end of the pool, and I got permission to take you with me." Elizabeth then laid out their mission and her plan to complete it.

"I have no problem with that. I had begun to think this job wasn't as exciting as I first thought it would be. Where do we start?" Poppy asked.

"I'd like to go to the Major's house first. I took you there before, but you didn't meet him. He is calmer and more level-headed than Rufus Lewis, but don't let that fool you."

Poppy couldn't help but wonder what she had just agreed to.

It took the rest of the day to put their plan together, which included getting an update on James Lewis' murder investigation. It seemed there wasn't any new information other than what she and Elizabeth had found out at what she now came to think of as 'The Stink Shop'.

So besides having a son who was murdered, it was now common knowledge that two of Rufus' other boys had been severely beaten by the same family he suspected of killing his youngest son. Although the Lewises hadn't reported this latest incident, it wouldn't go away. They knew it wasn't going to sit well with Rufus. Poppy told Elizabeth, 'The pot was boiling, and the lid was on tight. It wouldn't be long before it would blow off.' Everyone knew that progress had to be made quickly on the case.

CHAPTER 19

THE FAMILIES

The Major and his family typically met at his home on Sundays and caravanned to church together. But the Sunday after the Highway encounter, Margo questioned whether the McKay clan should attend church. The Major exploded.

"No one is going to dictate to me whether I should or should not attend the church I have belonged to for almost thirty years. We will attend church services as a family, and Rufus Lewis can be damned!"

Kurt had invited Poppy to attend Sunday services with him at Pastor Tilley's church at Burr Ferry. She gladly accepted, but not before jokingly asking him if he thought she could be related to the Pastor.

On the day of the service, he arrived at Poppy's house half an hour early. Kurt sat out front for a few minutes, straightening his bolo tie before turning the rearview mirror to examine his hair. Satisfied, he returned the mirror to its proper position and walked to Poppy's door. Just as he was ready to knock, she opened the door. He considered this a good sign, thinking she had been anxiously waiting for him. Kurt paused for a second, taking in her appearance; she was stunning. The sunlight gleamed off her long, dark hair while her brown eyes glistened as she stared at him.

"Are you okay, Kurt?" Poppy asked.

"Yes, I'm fine. I just…you look amazing," Kurt said.

They arrived at the church just as the service was about to begin. As they entered the door, they noticed Elizabeth and Jerry seated a couple of rows back from the pulpit. When Poppy walked down the aisle, she saw the entire McKay Clan sitting on the left side. She noticed the Lewis Family on the right side of the aisle. Poppy couldn't help thinking, *and never the twain shall meet*. Rufus looked up and took a glance at her. The sun coming through the window shone on his thick, curly beard, giving it a warm glow. For an instant, he had an angelic look about him, which softened his stern features. When Poppy looked closer, she saw he wasn't wearing his signature .44 Magnum pistol. She breathed a sigh of relief. She took in the congregation and knew immediately that no one could deny the tension in the church that morning, including Pastor Tilley. She slipped into the pew directly in front of the McKays and sat down next to Elizabeth and Jerry. She hoped that it didn't represent them as taking sides.

Pastor Tilley began the service hoping that his sermon on brotherly love would strike a positive emotion and touch the hearts of the Lewis and McKay families. Although both families listened intently to Pastor Tilley, they never made eye contact with each other. There was no immediate sign that the sermon had any effect on them. Even though he delivered a powerful message this morning, it appeared that it would have to simmer for a while before it had any impact.

The case of who killed his son and buried him on the McKay property still hadn't been solved. Rufus was sure that the Major didn't kill his son, but he couldn't put the thought out of his mind that one of the Major's people had done it—probably with the Major's knowledge and possibly his approval.

Two weeks after the Texas Highway beating had occurred, Rufus Lewis called a family meeting after Sunday dinner. Since Conor and Tanner had taken matters into their own hands by assaulting the Major's daughter-in-law on the highway, it had added fuel to an already simmering fire. He would address all of his sons and tell them he wanted no more stupidity. They were to do nothing without his knowledge and approval. But that didn't mean he would sit back and do nothing. Rufus was a spirited man with a volatile temper, but he wasn't stupid. He glared at his two sons. Conor's jaw was still wired shut, and both of Tanner's eyes were black and blue when Rufus called the family meeting to order.

"I want you all to look at those two idiots," Rufus said, pointing to the bruised boys. "See what happens when you do something without a plan." He turned and looked at the rest of the family before continuing. "You end up getting your brains kicked in."

He knew that getting into a shooting war or physical confrontation with the Major would be detrimental to him and his family. He decided to use the law to best the Major. Rufus planned to get an injunction against McKay, keeping him out of the river so the Lewis family could harvest the sinker logs. Oh, he knew that more than half the logs were on the Louisiana side, stuck in the sand and clay banks. The unspoken agreement was that Major McKay was entitled to the logs on the Louisiana side, and Rufus Lewis owned the logs on the Texas side. But it was Rufus' opinion that the majority of the logs were actually cut in Texas and drifted over to Louisiana. Because of a bend in the river, the logs had been impelled into the Louisiana river bank. He had already consulted an attorney who told him he had a good chance of winning this argument. He was going to find a solution in a Louisiana court for what he felt were his Texas logs.

CHAPTER 20

VISITING THE CRIME SCENE

Sheriffs Craft and Newman knew they needed to make progress on the James Lewis murder before it turned into a cold case. They agreed on who should work the case, too, but it would take some convincing of a couple of agencies outside their jurisdiction to make it happen. Bobby Craft decided to contact Tim O'Connor, the Vernon Parish District attorney, and ask if he could loan Poppy Nichols to the Sheriff's Department until the investigation ran its course. Hopefully, that course would be the conviction of whoever committed the crime. It was decided that the two of them would plead their case to the U.S. Marshall Service regarding 'borrowing' one of their U.S. Deputy Marshalls, Elizabeth Weaver. Part of their argument was that these two had already made more progress on this case than anyone else. They had already been given permission to work the accident on the Texas Highway, which would include a visit to the Major's home. Additionally, the fact that they were related to more than half the Parish was a big plus because folks didn't like talking to strangers. They were relieved when both agencies agreed to the arrangement.

When Poppy and Elizabeth were notified of their new assignment, they were elated to be given such a high-profile case but were also apprehensive. After all, with so many of their blood relatives living in this jurisdiction, they hoped the perpetrator wasn't related to them! The two women immediately sat down and tweaked their previous plan on how to tackle this new joint assignment. First, they retraced the previous investigators' steps and read through all the interviews. Once this was done, they agreed they should stick to their prior plan and start at Major McKay's property and the gravesite of James Lewis.

Poppy and Elizabeth arrived at the Major's home just before noon the following day. When they got out of the car, the chilly breeze off the river met them head-on, along with the smell of hickory smoke that filled their nostrils with a rich aroma as it wafted through the air. Poppy buttoned the top of her coat and looked at Elizabeth, who was doing the same thing. An old Walker hound lying on the porch stood up, looked at them, gave a couple of howls, and then lay back down as if his work for the day was done. Elizabeth approached the door and rang the doorbell. A dour Bonnie Blue opened the door. Although she courteously invited them in and offered them a seat, she was not chatty like she had been on their previous visit. Poppy asked Bonnie Blue if the Major was in just as Margo entered the room. Overhearing the question, she told them that the Major had left earlier for the horse barn with the intention of taking his morning ride on his new stallion, Blackstone. She led them out onto the front veranda and pointed toward a paved road, advising them that the barn was at the end of that road. Margo then exited the room just as quietly as she had come in. They didn't have time to thank her or question her.

They discussed the strange encounter as they got into their car and drove to the end of the winding road. Strange, because of Bonnie's behavior and because Margo never inquired what they wanted with the Major. They weren't assuming that Margo stuck her nose in his business, but this wasn't regular business; it was law enforcement business. It seemed odd that she wasn't just a little bit curious about why they were there. The drive was along a quarter-mile winding road that took them through cypress, oak, and pignut hickory trees. Most of the leaves had fallen, but the drive was still beautiful. They reached the barn and parked next to an ATV. Poppy and Elizabeth got out of their vehicle and walked toward the barn. Just as they reached the large opened double doors, the Major walked out of the tack room. They startled each other.

"Good morning, ladies. What brings you out here today?" The Major asked with a smile.

So, Margo didn't give him a 'heads-up' that they were coming down to the barn, Poppy thought, before advising the Major the reason for their visit. "Morning, Major. We were hopeful that you could lead us to the spot where James Lewis was found buried."

"Sure can, but can you tell me why the law wants to go back out there at this late date? Wouldn't the men who already investigated have gotten all that they need?" The Major asked.

There was no mistaking what the Major meant with this comment, but after looking at each other, Poppy and Elizabeth decided they wouldn't play his game.

Elizabeth got right to the point. "The investigation of young James' death has been assigned to us now with the hope that we can develop more leads. We're starting from ground zero, which means we need to examine the place where James Lewis' body was found buried. Rather than go trampling all over your property without permission, we thought you might take us there."

The Major knew there was no arguing that point and told them it would be best if they took his ATV as the ground gets kind of rugged back toward the river. It appeared they had a working arrangement!

Poppy and Elizabeth piled into the back of the ATV as the Major drove through some rough terrain. It was a good ten minutes before they approached the river's edge, and the ATV came to a stop.

Pointing to an area about one hundred feet ahead, the Major spoke up. "Ladies, you see that big red oak tree over there? Just to the left of that, about twenty feet, you will see where James was found." He paused for a moment, then pointed across the river where it flowed around a bend. "At the furthest tip of the protrusion is a large willow tree. See it?" The Major asked.

The women both nodded.

"The easternmost part of the state of Texas ends right here between Evans and Burr Ferry in Vernon Parish, Louisiana. If you go due west from this spot for eight hundred and fifty-six miles, you will find the western tip of Texas in El Paso. Just something I thought you would like to know. I'm returning to the ATV and waiting for you ladies to finish," the Major said with a smile. Let them get all muddy, he thought. He certainly didn't want to mess up his leather riding boots.

Poppy was walking ten feet from the site when the sun flashed across something shiny. She walked over to the object and looked down at it. Taking a plastic bag from her coat pocket, she called out to Elizabeth. Poppy pointed down to the object partially covered by a sycamore leaf. Picking it up by the edges, she carefully bagged it before they examined it. It was a large silver button, possibly from a coat or jacket. It had a large star stamped in the middle, similar to the star of Texas. Its size and weight were unusual—not something you'd see every day. They searched a while longer but didn't find anything else. Thinking this was a successful outing, they returned to the ATV, where the Major was waiting.

Poppy waited until they were settled back into their seats before asking the Major the question she and Elizabeth had settled on. "How cold does it get out here around August/September?"

"Oh, lord, it's still pretty darn hot around these parts at that time of year. Why do you ask?"

"Just curious, Sir."

"May I ask you a question, Ms. Nichols?"

"Sure," Poppy said.

"Are you ready for a gut-wrenching ride back to the barn?" The Major said with a laugh.

Their return to the barn, along the muddy logging trail, was just as rough as their original departure had been. When they arrived, Poppy and Elizabeth thanked the Major and left. Even though they knew anyone could have lost the button while fishing on the river bank, it was worth a shot to have it fingerprinted and checked to see if they could determine its origin. Although, if it came from an article of clothing worn in cooler weather, it probably had nothing to do with the crime scene. Since they had little else to go on, it might be worth some research time.

When Poppy and Elizabeth returned to the Sheriff's office, they wanted to review what they found with Sheriff Craft before logging it into the evidence room. Sticking her head into his office, Poppy asked for a minute of his time, and he agreed. She pulled out the evidence bag holding the button and showed it to the Sheriff.

"We found this button about ten feet from the James Lewis gravesite. Looks like it might be a coat button, but checking the weather at the time of James' death, I doubt it's connected. I wanted to get your input before discounting it."

"So, you found this at the gravesite?" Craft asked.

"Yes, Sir, Elizabeth and I did."

"Well, I can see how you'd mistake it for a button, but this here is a decorative medallion from a belt. They're pretty popular around here. Whoever lost it must have come in from the river. Otherwise, the McKays would have spotted them. That is unless it belonged to one of them, but I doubt it because the star on that medallion represents Texas," Craft said.

"You mean like the belts that have several going all the way around the waist? I hadn't thought of that. Thanks, Sheriff."

Poppy took the medallion to the fingerprint lab, and after recording it as evidence, she released it to them for processing. She knew it was a long shot since it had been out in the elements for several months. But she wanted to cover all her bases.

CHAPTER 21

DNA

Jack McKay, the Major's eldest son, was leaving the doctor's office in Leesville after receiving some unexpected news. The news wasn't just unexpected; it was overwhelming. He had only consulted the doctor at his mother's insistence after he had lost a disturbing amount of weight and felt fatigued more often than not. Along with these symptoms, he also had chills and muscle weakness, which were taking their toll. He didn't argue with his mother about the doctor's appointment because, to tell the truth, his symptoms scared even him. On his first visit, the doctor ordered bloodwork to see what was happening. When the results of his lab work were analyzed, they indicated it could be something serious. The doctor called and asked that he submit to more tests to see if his suspicion was correct, and Jack agreed. He would have to wait a bit longer for an answer. Today was the day he got that answer, and his head was spinning as he tried to fully digest it. The doctor confirmed that Jack had leukemia and had then gone over his options, advising that a bone marrow transplant would be the most successful. He had gone to the doctor alone today and wished he hadn't. He certainly didn't expect this type of news when he headed out the door. He needed to head home and talk to both of his parents. His mother would help him decide what to do next. She always had.

    The Major and Margo were devastated. The doctor had isolated the problem and put them in touch with the bone marrow registry, but no match was available. It looked like it was up to them to find a donor. A relative was the most likely candidate, so Jack's siblings were tested first. They were gutted when none of them were a match. The doctor then advised the McKays that they needed to look outside the family, perhaps way outside the family, to find a possible match. A donor might be challenging to find, but they weren't giving up. They would search the entire country if need be.

    The McKays contacted everyone they knew in Vernon and Beauregard Parish and asked if they would get tested to see if they were a match for their son, Jack. Most agreed, even those that weren't fond of the Major, because they had no beef with Jack. Sheriff Bobby Craft's and the District Attorney's offices were contacted and asked to put out the word that the McKays were asking for volunteers.

Elizabeth and Poppy were in the breakroom when the Sheriff's administrative assistant came in and announced the need for people to be tested. They looked at each other and said, 'Why not?' The next day, Poppy, Elizabeth, and several deputies walked the three blocks to the clinic, where the testing was being done. The samples were sent off to a lab in Baton Rouge. The cousins felt they had done a good deed but didn't expect anything to come of it.

The McKays had gotten the word out, and at last count, they knew of over 2,000 people who had been tested. They knew this wasn't a large number in the grand scheme of things—but it only took one match. They were elated when they got the call from the registry. A match had been found! Jack and Margo wasted no time making arrangements to meet with the Registry's Donor Coordinator.

Jack and his mother nervously waited for the nurse to call him into the office. They wondered how good a match they had found and if that person was willing to be a donor. It was one thing asking someone to get tested, but going through with the donation required quite the commitment on the donor's part. Not to mention the recovery period. Jack held his breath when he was called, and the door closed behind him.

"Good morning, Jack. We have some great news. We have found a very close familial match. I'm guessing this sibling wasn't available for testing when the rest of your family first tested?" She asked.

Jack looked confused. "All of my immediate and extended family tested right away once I was diagnosed. Could the Registry have missed it?"

"From what I see here, the match was found with the most recent round of testing we received. According to the DNA profile, the matched sample belongs to your sister," the nurse replied.

"I don't understand. My sister, Bonnie Blue, was tested, and we weren't a match," Jack said.

"This sample didn't belong to her; it was from your other sister," the nurse said.

"What other sister?" Jack asked.

"It shows here that it's your sister, Poppy Nichols."

Jack sat back in his chair in complete shock. He was thrilled to find a match, but to be told that Poppy was his sister? How? Why? "The lab must be mistaken. Don't get me wrong, I'm thrilled that we've got a match, but the lab must have mismarked the DNA," Jack said.

"I'm reading the report, and there's no mistake. The name on the test sample is Poppy Nichols, and the DNA count shows 2,436 cMs, which is indicative of a sister. Well, it could also represent a half-sister, but no more distant than that," came the reply.

Jack was quiet, then thanked her before asking what was next. She explained that they had to contact the donor and let her know she was a match. From there, it was just paperwork until a date was set for the procedure. He would have another appointment before the transplant along with the donor so they could educate them both on what to expect. Jack thanked her, walked back into the waiting room, and told his mother he was ready to go.

The nurse coordinator couldn't help but feel she had done something wrong. It certainly came as a surprise to the patient that the donor match was related to him. She thought she had possibly made a mistake by not contacting the donor first, but all donors signed a disclosure agreeing that once they tested, there was no right to privacy. If they were a match, it would be divulged to the patient. The other part she hadn't told Jack was that sometimes the difficult part was securing the donor's approval for the transplant. Most weren't aware that their life would be disrupted for a bit. But typically, they agreed once all the steps of the procedure were broken down for them.

Margo looked at Jack and knew that something was wrong. "Jack, are you okay? Is there a problem with the match? Do I need to go back in and speak with the coordinator?"

"I'm pleased about the match, Mom. I was told I'm lucky because my sister and I matched," Jack said, irritated.

"That doesn't make sense, Jack. Bonnie Blue and you didn't match. I saw the test results myself."

"That's right, Mom, we didn't. It was my other sister that I matched with—Poppy Nichols! Is there something you want to tell me?"

Margo sat in the car in shock as Jack drove. She could see his tight grip on the steering wheel. She stared out the window and wondered how to explain this. Heck, the Major didn't even know. It had been so long ago, almost twenty-eight years. She had been in love with Louis Nichols, but that love was unrequited. Jack was the only thing she had left of that love, and he was precious to her. She knew she owed him the truth and asked him to pull over.

Margo sat quietly for a minute before she reached back in time to a place that she had not revisited in years. She turned to Jack and told him her story.

She met Emmitt McKay at the beginning of her junior year in college. They dated all the way through graduation, when Emmitt asked her to marry him. She accepted, and the plan was for Emmitt to go into the Marine Corps upon graduation, and they would marry when he received his first leave. She moved to Emmitt's parent's home on the Sabine River during that time. She told Jack that she loved Emmitt but was never in love with him. But they got along well, and he offered her a promising future. Much better than she could have expected if she had returned to her hometown after graduation.

There was very little to do in Burr Ferry—especially for a young adult. So, she frequented the Catfish House down by the

Sabine River Bridge. Back then, it was the only place for young adults to hang out. One night, she was gossiping with her newly made friends when a tall, attractive man came in. Everyone seemed to know him, and he was friendly to everyone, including her. She couldn't take her eyes off of him. Margo had to know more, so she asked one of the girls who he was. She told her that he had already been taken. He was engaged to one of the local girls, Abby James, who happened to be away at college. Margo couldn't help but think that they had a lot in common. She was also engaged, but her fiancé was away serving our country. She took a breath and wiped her eyes.

"I saw him again a week later and decided to start a conversation with him right then and there. He was the politest and best-looking man I had ever seen. I saw him a couple more times after that. The next time, I asked him out. By that time, I was totally in love with him. We were out one night, parked by the river, and things went too far. Afterward, I told him I was in love and wanted to marry him. He told me he was in love with someone else, and they were to be married. That was the end of the relationship, and it broke my heart. Eight weeks later, Emmitt came home on leave. I knew I was pregnant but didn't tell him. We followed through on our original plan and got married. You were born thirty-two weeks later." Margo finished and looked over at Jack.

He sat in the driver's seat, staring straight ahead as if frozen. His mind was racing so fast that he was almost dizzy.

"Does dad know?"

"I don't know. We never talked about it, so I assumed that he didn't. He's always treated you the same as the other children," Margo said.

"Well, Poppy is going to know soon enough."

"I know. It would be best if you spoke to her first before the Registry contacts her. As soon as you drop me off, you should turn around and go back to Leesville. She needs to hear this from you." She had always given Poppy the cold shoulder and didn't want to be the one to tell her why. Margo had no problem sending her son to do her bidding! She'd always been a coward.

Jack did as his mother suggested, and thirty minutes later, he was sitting in front of the Vernon Parish Sheriff's office. It took him another five minutes to get his courage up enough to walk through the door. When he walked in, he saw Deputy Paul Yeary at the front desk and asked if Poppy was in. He gave Jack a nod and paged Poppy, asking her to come to the front.

"Hey Jack, what brings you here today? If it's about the testing, me and several others have already been to the clinic."

"Yes, Poppy, I know. Can we possibly talk in your office?"

She was puzzled but motioned for him to follow her. They entered her office, and Jack took a seat.

"What's wrong, Jack? Have you had bad news? Is no one that tested a match?" Poppy asked.

"I take it you haven't had a call from the clinic yet. Maybe I shouldn't do this here. Can we meet when you get off work?"

"Jack, you're here now. Just tell me what's on your mind, and we'll deal with it."

Jack blurted out. "We are a match, Poppy."

"That's wonderful news, Jack. I'm so glad I could help you. Are you here because you're concerned that I won't go through with the transplant?" Poppy asked.

"No, Poppy, that's not it. There's more, much more."

Poppy sat up. He had her attention now. What could it be that had Jack looking so glum?

"Jack, I won't bite. Start at the beginning and tell me what has you so upset."

"Poppy, when the lab results came back and showed you as a match, it also showed you are my sister. I asked if it could be a mistake, and they told me that wasn't possible. Since finding out, I've spoken to my mother. She has confirmed that we have the same father."

She sat quietly for a few seconds and looked at him.

Jack sat in the chair, wondering if he had made a mistake by coming here. He should have let the nurse coordinator deliver the news to Poppy. Her silence was unnerving.

Then, he saw her break out with a big smile.

"You're him! I just knew you still lived here in Vernon Parish. I just knew it!"

Jack looked at her, puzzled, but then he also started smiling.

Poppy got up from her chair, walked around her desk, and hugged Jack. "You're my brother. Do you realize that since my parents are deceased, you're my closest relative in the world? I'm so glad to find out it was you, Jack."

"You knew you had a brother? Apparently, you know more than I do. How did you find out? And when did you find out?" Jack asked incredulously.

Taking Jack's hands in hers, she told him she had been gifted her mother's journal recently, and by reading it, she learned she had a brother. She wanted to find him but was concerned the search would damage her biological brother's family.

And there it was! Jack grew up thinking that the Major was his biological father. Revealing this now would no doubt cause hurt for all involved. After some discussion, Poppy and Jack decided to keep it quiet. Of course, this being Vernon Parish, there probably wasn't a chance in hell of that happening. They both had the same thought, 'How was the Major going to handle this news?'

When Margo returned home, she didn't stop but headed directly into the Major's study. He was sitting behind his desk reviewing some paperwork. He peered over his glasses when he heard her walk in. By the look on her face, he knew something was wrong. It was almost a grimace as she pulled a chair up to his desk. He hoped it wasn't bad news regarding a match for Jack's transplant. The Major removed his glasses and placed them on a spreadsheet he had been reading.

"What is it, Margo, that can't wait?" The Major asked.

"It's about Jack, Emmitt."

"Did something go wrong at the clinic this morning? I knew they found a donor, and it was a good match, right?"

"No, there's nothing wrong with the match, just with who the donor is, or would be, if she agrees to the transplant," Margo replied.

"I'm confused, Margo. Did Poppy Nichols say no to the transplant?"

Margo's head spun around, and she looked at the Major head-on. "You knew who the donor was before I had a chance to tell you? Did Jack call you?"

"I knew about the match ten minutes after the results arrived at the clinic. I know everything that involves this family almost as soon as it happens."

"I should have realized that, Emmitt. I wish you had said something before Jack and I left for the clinic this morning. It would have been less of a shock. To answer your question about Ms. Nichols, I don't know how she feels about being a donor. Jack was on his way to her office to have a discussion with her. But there's more I need to talk to you about regarding Jack and Poppy Nichols," Margo said.

The Major held up the palm of his right hand to silence her. Margo stopped in mid-sentence.

"Margo, I know all about Jack's biological father and have known for years. I can do the math. I'm not stupid. Jack was born early, and he wasn't a preemie. No matter what, Jack is my son, and anyone who says differently will have to deal with me. I was in love with Jack at first sight, Margo. Just as I was with you. We were a happy family—there was no reason to ruin it. I decided we didn't need to discuss it between us or anyone else."

Neither Margo nor the Major heard Bonnie Blue come into the room.

"You mean Jack has another sister besides me?" Bonnie Blue asked.

They turned to see her standing in the doorway of the Major's study and wondered how much she had heard. Apparently, enough to ascertain that Jack and Poppy were brother and sister.

"Since she is Jack's sister, does that mean she's part of our family? I'd like that. Poppy is intelligent and professional, and she's stunning. I like her a lot!" Bonnie exclaimed.

The Major spoke first. "Technically, only she and Jack are related, But I don't have a problem bringing her into the clan."

Bonnie Blue looked at her mother questioningly.

"Yes, Bonnie, when she comes to see us, I will play nice and welcome her. I don't want to cause friction in this family. Major, I know word of this will get around. How am I supposed to handle the looks, not to mention the questions?"

"Well, Margo, you created this situation; it's yours to clean up. Just remember you have other children besides Jack. Don't embarrass them." Then, the Major raised his hand and waved them out of his office. He stared at the wall momentarily as in deep thought and then returned to the work on his desk.

CHAPTER 22

ELIZABETH AND JERRY

It was a welcomed, brisk autumn morning in Leesville, and Elizabeth decided to take advantage of it. The summer heat had been brutal this year. As she walked down Third Street, she could feel the chill on her face. She enjoyed it but still turned her jacket collar up to block the wind. People she met on the sidewalk greeted her warmly with 'Good morning, Marshall Weaver', and 'Good day, Elizabeth.' She couldn't help but smile at the familiarity. Growing up in Dallas, most people were as chilly as the autumn breeze she enjoyed this morning. She was in a very good mood, and nothing could wipe the smile off her face. She and Jerry were going on what he called a 'formal' date tonight. This was not a date camouflaged as a business lunch or meeting but a proper date with a man she deeply cared for. Elizabeth knew the importance of keeping their relationship secret in the early stages. But as their relationship evolved, they felt comfortable making public how they felt for each other. Jerry had arranged the details of this date, which he hadn't shared with her. Oh, except that he did tell her to 'dress nice.' She knew what that meant in Dallas but wasn't sure how that translated in this part of the country. Her thoughts were on Jerry, and before she knew it, she was standing in front of the Sheriff's Office and hardly remembered walking there.

When she walked in, the desk deputy greeted her and smiled; she returned his greeting with a 'Good morning, Marcus.' Elizabeth walked down the hallway to her office and stopped when she saw Jerry sitting in a chair beside her desk, his head buried in a folder full of paperwork. He looked up at her and smiled.

"Good morning, beautiful," Jerry said with his infectious smile.

Not only was she surprised to see him in her office, but she was startled by how he had greeted her. Their relationship was out in the open now, so there was no need to hide how they felt. She smiled right back at him and wished him a good morning, too. She liked this new dynamic. In fact, she liked it a lot!

Jerry shared with her that he had been up in the northwestern part of the parish doing an unrelated investigation and had discovered that Marley Powell was back. Jerry wasn't sure of his exact location, but his sources told him that Marley was staying with his uncle a few miles west of the small town of Hornbeck. Elizabeth took the file from Jerry's hand and placed it on her desk. Work was the furthest thing from her mind right now.

She looked at him and asked. "Where are you taking me tonight?"

"I was hoping you liked Italian food."

"It's one of my favorite food groups!" Elizabeth said, laughing.

"Great. I'll pick you up at 7:00 tonight. I guessed you were a pasta kind of girl, so I already made a reservation at *Rita's Broadway Italian Restaurant*. I hope that's okay with you."

"Yes, that's perfect."

As Jerry was leaving, he touched the back of her hand and then squeezed it.

Elizabeth liked Jerry before, but she loved this new version of Jerry. What he didn't know was that a peanut butter and jelly sandwich eaten on a park bench would have been fine with her as long as Jerry was there. What she probably didn't know was that he felt the same.

Elizabeth had just finished getting ready for her date when she heard a knock on the door. She looked at the clock on the mantle, saw it was 6:45 p.m., and wondered if it could be Jerry. Not only on time but early? She opened the door after peeking out the window and confirming it was him. There stood Jerry dressed in a suit. Elizabeth had only seen him dressed like this a few times, and that was in court. Boy, this must be a special occasion, she thought. I feel like he's picking me up for prom night.

Ten minutes later, they were arriving at *Rita's.* Once they were seated the small talk began. Dinner was splendid, and Jerry had pre-ordered dessert. Rita, who owned the restaurant, came out with a large piece of Italian Wedding Cake, expresso, and two forks. Rita smiled as she placed the cake and coffee on the table. The night couldn't have gone any better, and now she was being served this delicious cake.

"What's the special occasion?" Elizabeth asked.

Jerry asked her if she realized that they had actually known each other for almost two years. They had breakfast, lunches, and dinners together. They worked hand in hand during that time and spent more time together than each spent separately at home. Then, turning serious, he took her hand and told her. "I'm turning 41 years old next week. I haven't had someone close to me since my mother died over twenty years ago. I don't know if you realized it, but I have loved you since we first met."

Elizabeth's heart was pounding. It felt like it would beat right out of her chest. What is he doing? She thought.

Jerry reached into his jacket pocket and pulled out a small black box. Elizabeth thought maybe it was earrings, but her birthday had passed, and Christmas was still a few months away. The suspense was killing her, but she didn't have to wait long. He opened the box, and inside sat a three-carat diamond engagement ring. Elizabeth was stunned. She looked at the ring in complete surprise and couldn't speak. He couldn't interpret the look she gave him. Her silence and facial expression showed no clue how she felt. Was she happy, or was this a bad idea? Since she was quiet, he could only speak up and tell her more about his feelings.

"Elizabeth, I don't want to be alone anymore. As I've gotten to know you, I realized that you were someone I want to spend the rest of my life with. What I'm asking here is, will you marry me?" Jerry asked.

Elizabeth looked at him, and she still couldn't form a word. She just nodded her head. He stood up, went to her chair, and kissed her; then he put the ring on her finger. Elizabeth held her hand up and studied it as she thought I'm going to be Mrs. Lambert. Then she spoke for the first time since he had whipped out the jewelry box.

"That ring looks perfect on my finger like it's always belonged there, doesn't it, Jerry?"

Now it was his turn to just nod. Jerry couldn't speak without the chance that he would become emotional. Elizabeth whispered under her breath. 'I'm going to be Mrs. Jerry Lambert.'

CHAPTER 23

THE WEEKEND

When the alarm sounded, Poppy rolled over and turned it off. She rubbed the sleep out of her eyes and then remembered why she had set her alarm for six-thirty on her day off. This Saturday morning, she had plans to take her horse, Peggy, for an early morning ride at the O'Shea Ranch. She glanced through the partially opened curtain and saw the sun coming up. Poppy pulled the curtain back further and noticed frost on the window. Better bundle up for this ride, she said under her breath. As she was pouring her second cup of coffee, her phone rang. She looked at the screen and saw it was Kurt. This brought a smile to Poppy's face, and she answered his call right away. She had liked him from the first time she saw him at Pearl Creek, even though it was an embarrassing situation. Of course, he had seen more of her than she of him. Thinking back on it conjured up a laugh. She couldn't help but feel that the more she was around him, the more she wanted to be with Kurt. She was becoming very attracted to him. It wasn't just his rugged good looks; his warm personality had a way of drawing you in.

"Good morning, Kurt."

"Morning, Poppy. It's a chilly one. Make sure you wear something warm."

"I had planned on it, but thanks for the reminder. I'll see you in half an hour."

When Poppy arrived at the ranch, it was even colder. Funny how these cooler temperatures crept up on you. She walked to the stall where Peggy was stabled and saw someone had already saddled her. Poppy grabbed the reins and led her to the paddock where Kurt was saddling his horse, Buck. He looked at her and smiled, then pointed toward a ridge about a mile away.

"We're riding up there," Kurt said.

Poppy nodded.

The ride up to the ridge was brisk, but the wind chill didn't matter as long as she was riding with Kurt. When they got to the top of the ridge, Kurt pointed to the north. They were looking down on a large lake that seemed to go forever.

"We are looking at Lake Vernon. If you look to the northwest, you will see a cabin on a knoll overlooking the lake. It belongs to me and my sister. I didn't rent out the cabin for this winter. If you're up for a little cold-weather fishing, it's all ours for any weekend you like."

"Moving a little fast, aren't you, cowboy?" Poppy said with a laugh.

"It's a two-bedroom and two-bath cabin," Kurt said, smiling.

There was no mistaking it now. Kurt was interested, and Poppy couldn't be happier. They rode for another hour and returned to the stable. During the ride back, Poppy told Kurt that a weekend fishing trip sounded great. He gave her a broad smile.

After arranging the time, Poppy went home and packed an overnight bag, then returned to the ranch to meet Kurt. She was excited about this trip because it afforded her some time to get to know him better. So far, she liked what she saw, but she hoped to get a good sense of how he thought and felt towards the rest of the world. That was important to her. Although, so far, she knew he had a good heart. This weekend, she would not concentrate on a McKay and Lewis feud and certainly not Marley Powell. She decided there would be no work, just relaxing and fishing with a handsome cowboy.

Elizabeth had just gotten out of the shower when her phone rang. Seeing the caller ID, she became excited because it was Jerry. Looking at her nightstand, she saw it was just 9:05 a.m. She answered on the first ring and heard a cheerful voice on the other end.

"How about breakfast at the Ranch House Café? I can be over in twenty minutes." Jerry said.

"Perfect," was her reply.

Within twenty minutes, Elizabeth heard a knock on her door. Thinking it was Jerry, she threw the door open with enthusiasm. However, to her surprise, standing there was her neighbor, Johnny Jean. He didn't miss her frown when she saw it was him.

"Good morning, Elizabeth. It seems you had an unwanted visitor last night. I was walking Max this morning and saw you have flats, as in all of your tires are flat!"

Elizabeth walked out to her U.S. Marshall's car and saw that, without a doubt, all of her tires were deflated. Just as she was inspecting the vandalism, Jerry drove up. He walked over to the car and peered at the damage.

"This doesn't look good," he said. "All four of your tires have been stabbed in the sidewalls. This isn't random vandalism. I think it was some type of warning. Elizabeth, I'd prefer it if you came with me until we can get this sorted out. How long will it take you to pack a bag?" Jerry asked.

Elizabeth wasted no time calling a tow truck to have the vehicle hauled in for new tires. Then she moved her personal car to Jerry's apartment, where she would stay until she could get a handle on who caused the vandalism. She and Jerry discussed the suspects who could have a vendetta against her. One name kept coming to mind: Marley Powell. He knew the name of every law enforcement officer who was at the shootout at his uncle's house. Marley also knew who had served the warrant. Law enforcement was aware that he was back in the northwest part of Vernon Parish, where his relatives were hiding him. Everyone in that part of the parish was afraid of the Powells and knew that there would be repercussions if they informed on him. She knew it was a good place to start but decided not to do anything until Monday. She didn't want it to ruin her weekend.

    Jerry had planned a weekend at a cabin he had rented on Toledo Bend Lake. The sun was just beginning to set over the lake when they arrived. They got out of the car, walked to the water's edge, and watched as the bright glow from the sun turned the water a reddish-orange. They watched the last moments of the sun disappearing behind the trees on the west side of the lake. Jerry pointed to a flock of geese passing between the clouds surrounding the sun's last glow of the day. In the distance, geese flew in a V formation, honking and giving off a serene sound that echoed across the water. Elizabeth smiled, took his hand, and gently squeezed. Jerry looked at her and gave her a warm smile. The soft radiance of the setting sun hovered over Jerry's face, projecting a beautiful profile. He took Elizabeth, pulled her close, and kissed her. She never wanted this moment to end. Jerry was feeling the same way.

CHAPTER 24

THE GOLD COINS

For two months after the disastrous raid on his brother's house, Marley Powell had been hiding out at his uncle's, west of the small town of Hornbeck. The property was located in a heavily forested area, and the locals knew he was there and wouldn't give up his location for a couple of reasons. The first was that most had known him since birth and were probably related to him, and the second was because they were afraid of him. His reputation as a thief was well known, and some suspected him to be guilty of much worse crimes. They were also sympathetic about the death of his family members and felt what was left of the family had suffered enough. Either way, he was safe in this wooded hideaway from the U.S.

Marshal and the Sheriff's Department. He wasn't taking any chances traveling by road in Vernon Parish. Instead, he traveled by boat—one he had hidden in a cove on the Toledo Bend Lake. This large lake divided Louisiana and Texas much like the Sabine River did. He needed a safe mode of travel because he was now working full-time for Nick Durant fencing stolen property. It was the only means of making money that he had right now, what with the law after him. And the money was good, especially with what he skimmed off the top.

Marley had a meeting in Bon Wier, Texas, with Nick and his boys this evening, so he took the boat out and crossed the lake to the Texas side. He had stashed an old car there that he used as his mode of travel once he reached the Texas side of the lake. He felt safe driving in Cypress County because the U.S. Marshall that was after him was based out of Leesville, Louisiana.

It was early evening when Marley arrived at Nick Durant's office. He wasn't sure what Nick wanted him to sell, but he had mentioned that it would be very lucrative, which got Marley's attention. He parked his car in the alley and walked into the building through the back door, making his way down a short hallway to the shabby conference room. The smell of stale cigarette smoke assaulted him as soon as he walked into the room. Marley looked around at the mismatched chairs and the guys sitting around the long oak table with varnish peeling off and initials carved in it. He couldn't help but think what a bunch of born losers they all were. He took a seat in a chair with a loose leg that wiggled back and forth whenever you moved. He looked to his right and saw Nick's chief enforcer, Max Bren, who everyone knew was simple-minded. Marley laughed at the thought of him enforcing anything. Next to Nick was Pete Seaux. Pete was small but powerful, and Marley knew he was no idiot and dangerous. Pete was worth keeping an eye on.

"Bout time you made it, Marley. We have a lot to cover, and we have a room full of goods to move," Nick called out as soon as he took his seat.

"Well, I'm here now, Nick. Go for it," Marley said.

Durant's guys had just brought him several pieces of stolen jewelry, antique coins, and handguns that came from several burglaries in the Houston area. This was the biggest haul he had handled in quite a while, and he needed to get it sold. Nick had laid out a lot of money for these goods and wanted to be reimbursed quickly. People in his business didn't issue credit. It was cash on the barrel head. Marley started salivating when Nick spread out the jewelry and guns for their appraisal. He would be more than happy to fence this property. He could skim ten percent off the top minimum with a haul like this.

"Marley, you still got that connection in Texarkana, the one that handles rare coins?" Nick Durant asked.

"I sure do, and he's ready to go," Marley answered.

"Good because I have something special that only a collector might appreciate." Nick then gave the nod to Max.

Max went down the hallway to Nick's office to retrieve the 'special' item. A wooden box with a loose-fitting lid sat on the top of Nick's desk. He bent down to pick it up, but curiosity got the best of him. Max opened the lid, thinking it wouldn't hurt if he looked inside. He was staring at several coins, some shiny, some not, but one coin in particular caught his attention. It was the size of a half-dollar and had a painted picture of a soldier parachuting with the encryption *Death From Above* on the one side. He picked it up, turned it over, and saw a name, *Major Chuck Hampton*, on the other side. He held it for a minute, smiled, then put the coin in his pocket. He didn't think Nick would notice it missing; if he did, he probably wouldn't mind. Max figured he could always give it back if Nick said anything. He considered the coin his. Max had no idea it was a personalized U.S. Army challenge coin from the 101st Airborne. All he knew was that it was shiny, and he liked the look and feel of it when he held it.

Bren brought in the large wooden box, which, when opened, contained a very large pile of coins. Nick wasn't sure of their exact worth, but he guessed it was around one hundred thousand dollars in street value. Marley leaned over the box and picked up a few coins to examine. Some coins looked like they had come from a shipwreck—old and probably

Roman. He was sure they were the real deal. There was no mistaking the shiny glint of the gold coins on the bottom of the box. Digging down below, he picked up a couple of them. He was positive they were rare gold American coins.

"Do you think your guy would pay a hundred G's for the whole lot? I don't want to sell them piecemeal because I need them sold quickly. I want to make my money back, and I have expenses."

Marley thought he knew the worth of most of these coins at a glance; the total was way more than one hundred thousand dollars! A lot more. He assured Nick that it wouldn't be a problem. He could get these coins sold at his asking price and could have the money in less than ten days if that worked. Nick thought about it before handing the coins over to Marley. He previously had doubts about the guy, but Pete hadn't found any evidence that Marley had cheated him. He was going to have to have faith on this one. Handing the box over to Marley, he reiterated that he couldn't sell them for a penny under the hundred thousand dollar asking price and was holding him to the ten-day sale date.

Marley was elated as he snatched up the coins. It was obvious that Nick had no idea how much these coins were actually worth. He thought, okay, new plan here. Marley knew there was no way the guy in Texarkana could handle this quality and quantity of coins. But there was someone in Dallas who could. That ten percent he was going to take off the top went out the window. The true worth of these coins was closer to half a million dollars, and he would keep it all. That would be enough money to get him the heck out of Louisiana and a fresh start someplace else. It would also buy him plenty of companionship, which he hadn't had in quite a while. Let Nick go back to stealing goats and milk cows, he thought as he laughed to himself.

A week later, Marley arrived in Dallas with the gold coins. His buyer owned a chain of pawn shops across the country, but the coins weren't destined for these shops. This was a savvy buyer who knew he couldn't legitimately unload the stolen coins over the counter. But his underground connections were endless, and he'd have no trouble selling them if they were the quality Marley had told him they were. They were about to find out. The pawn shop owner looked at each coin, priced it individually, and told him the retail value was just over two million dollars. He told Marley he would give him five hundred and fifty thousand dollars for the lot and that he would give him half the money upfront. He had to wait for the balance of the money—it would be another two weeks before he could come up with the rest. Marley didn't like the terms of the deal and offered him half the coins. The pawn shop owner was not happy with the compromise but agreed to the arrangement.

"I'll give you two weeks to come up with the rest of the money. If my phone doesn't ring, I'll sell the remaining coins elsewhere. You understand?" Marley asked.

The buyer nodded, and Marley left for Louisiana.

Marley knew he needed to hear back from this guy as he had no other connections. At least no one that could handle this large of a purchase. Looking at the bright side, he did have two-hundred and twenty-five thousand dollars cash on him and half the coins. The less-than-bright side was that he knew if Nick didn't hear from him soon, he would come looking for him. Let him come to northwest Vernon Parish and try to collect! Marley laughed to himself as he pictured that Bon Wier, Texas, redneck threatening a Powell.

CHAPTER 25

THE LAKE

Elizabeth was packing the last sweater in her overnight bag when she heard a knock at the door. The rap, rap, rap noise brought a smile to her face. It was going to be another wonderful weekend spent with Jerry at the cabin on the Toledo Bend Lake. It had been a month since their last weekend fishing trip, and she had been anxious for another trip since. They loved the getaway and privacy the lake cabin afforded them. It didn't hurt that they both loved fishing and placing a bet on who would land the biggest bass or Bluegill perch. This would be their fourth trip, and so far, Elizabeth was leading two to one in the biggest fish category. She didn't let Jerry forget she was also leading in the most fish caught, three to zero. Fishing wasn't all that she loved about their trips. She enjoyed the bouncing of the boat caused by the waves and the mist it conjured up that sprayed in her face. She also liked looking at Jerry as he piloted the boat and watching the wind as it tousled his thick blond hair. He always had that infectious smile that melted her heart and that weak-in-the-knees feeling that came over her.

"Come in, Jerry. The door is open."

"Are you ready to be beaten in all fishing categories this weekend?" Jerry asked with a grin, walking over to assist with her bag.

"You can try, big boy, but it doesn't mean you will win," Elizabeth said, putting her arms around his neck and kissing him.

It was a forty-five-minute drive to the cabin and a pleasant one no matter the season. Along the way, Elizabeth stared out the window. She was caught up in her thoughts as she watched the trees, which now were almost void of leaves, pass by. The winter cold had changed the lush landscape into a stick forest, but she was still drawn to it. She guessed that was because it was so different from living in Dallas proper.

She and Jerry had not set a date for the wedding, and she thought this would be the perfect time to discuss plans for their nuptials. She smiled as she thought about her upcoming trip to Dallas with Poppy, which would be two-fold. She would finally meet Elizabeth's mother and they were going to shop for a wedding dress. The excitement and anticipation of the big day were too much to hold back. She leaned over and kissed Jerry on the cheek. He looked at her and smiled.

"And what was that for?"

"Oh, just because," Elizabeth said, looking into his sparkling blue eyes.

When they exited the truck at the cabin, the wind off the lake had a biting chill. She turned her collar up to protect her ears from the frigid cold. Jerry looked toward the lake and saw the waves were relatively high. Glancing at the boathouse, they saw the twenty-two-foot fishing boat being tossed around as the waves bounced it up and down like a child's toy.

"This is no day to be on the lake," Jerry said, as he opened the cabin door.

"You're right. Let's start a fire in the fireplace and get the chill out of the cabin."

Elizabeth pulled back the curtains from the large picture window that faced the lake. It seemed the wind had picked up, and was howling around the house. She looked at the large temperature gauge attached to a pole just outside the front door. The temperature registered 22°. What a weekend to pick to go fishing. The weatherman had promised much milder weather. She thought he must have been reporting from Key West, Florida, and not Vernon Parish. She glanced over at Jerry and saw that he had started a roaring fire. The heat from the fireplace was warming the cabin up quickly. It felt good on her ice-cold face. Jerry looked at her and smiled as he already had his boots off and was warming his feet in front of the fire.

He looked at her and sounded a big "Ahhh."

"What do you think the weather will be like tomorrow, Jerry?"

He whipped out his cell phone and looked up the weather report for the next day.

"Well, according to the *Whoop-de-doo Weatherman*, it will warm up, and the winds will lessen tomorrow, and it should be a balmy 32°," Jerry said with a laugh.

The following day, Elizabeth awoke to the smell of coffee wafting into the bedroom and the aroma of hickory-cured bacon frying in a pan. Next came the unmistakable scent of pancakes that enveloped her senses. She got out of bed, threw on a heavy robe, and made her way into the kitchen. She sure hoped it wasn't her mind playing tricks on her. She was definitely in the mood for a big breakfast. Jerry looked up as she walked in and sat at the kitchen island. He shoved a hot stack of pancakes and crispy bacon under her nose. Next came a vessel of maple syrup and softened butter. She looked at him and smiled as she dug into the breakfast.

Jerry looked at Elizabeth and asked, "Is there anything else I can do for you."

Elizabeth pushed the plate aside, leaned across the island, and said, "Yes, there is; you can go into the bathroom and warm up that toilet seat," she laughed.

The sun was just rising when Jerry and Elizabeth got in the boat. They had made the mutual decision to fish today regardless of the weather. It wasn't as cold as yesterday until Jerry pulled out of the wind-free cove and entered the open water on the lake. He gunned the motor, and the wind chill from the freezing temperature caused their faces to go numb. The frigid spray and mist from the boat bouncing over the waves added to her misery. And to think this was one part of fishing Elizabeth typically loved. She realized her enjoyment of the outdoor elements didn't apply to cold weather. But she put on a happy face, looked at Jerry, and smiled as she turned her collar up and buttoned it around her throat. Next, she pulled her woolen watch cap down over her ears.

"Do you think the fish will bite in this weather?" She asked, shivering.

Jerry answered loudly so he could be heard over the roar of the motor. "I have no idea. You're the expert fisherman," he laughed.

They had traveled fifteen minutes when Elizabeth saw what appeared to be someone broken down. The boater was standing on the back of the craft, working on the outboard motor and attempting to get it started. She motioned to Jerry and pointed toward the stranded fisherman. Jerry slowed the boat down and idled to the disabled craft. The man's back was turned to them as they pulled up beside the boat.

"Need some help?" Jerry asked.

Just as Jerry spoke, the man's engine sputtered to life. Then he turned to see who was offering him help and saw Elizabeth. They both had a spark of recognition at the same time. She recognized this man as the wanted fugitive, Marley Powell. Although shocked, she grabbed her bag and went for her Glock pistol. Marley reached under his coat and pulled his weapon, but Elizabeth fired first, ripping through Marley's coat and hitting the fleshy part of his shoulder. He returned fire, missing Elizabeth. Jerry had responded slower and was still trying to retrieve his weapon from his fishing tackle box when he was hit. Marley jumped behind the steering wheel of the now running boat, held his shoulder where he'd been shot, and sped off at full speed, heading west toward Texas.

Jerry's wound was to his right side, where it got him in the lung. Elizabeth immediately saw his labored breathing and went into action. She knew he had a sucking chest wound, having seen them before. Ripping off his jacket and shirt, she immediately put a patch over the wound and covered him with a blanket she had in the boat. It was essential to keep him as warm as possible. Elizabeth wasted no time trying to get aid to Jerry. She called for an ambulance and asked that they meet her at the closest landing, which was five minutes away. She kept talking to him while she steered the boat toward the landing. He smiled up at her, and then he reached for her hand. Elizabeth bent over and grasped his hand in hers. She recognized the signs as she felt his grip weakening and quickly realized he was going into shock.

"Hold on, Jerry, hold on." She pleaded as tears streamed down her face.

Jerry smiled weakly at her.

It seemed forever before she arrived at the landing, where the ambulance awaited them. The paramedics began working frantically on Jerry before putting him in the back of the ambulance. Elizabeth jumped in the back to ride with him. No way was she going to let him face this alone.

Fifteen minutes later, when they arrived at the hospital, Jerry was still conscious. He was rushed into the emergency room, where a thoracic surgeon was waiting. The nurses rushed Jerry down the hallway to an operating room. All the while, Elizabeth was holding his hand, talking to him, and begging him not to die. He looked up at her one last time and smiled before she let go of his hand. His fate was now in this unknown doctor's hands, along with God. She stood at the large double doors and watched as he was wheeled into the operating theater. She stood there momentarily paralyzed. Elizabeth was numb, and she began to pray and cry.

It took her several minutes to calm herself and make the necessary calls. The first call was to Poppy, then to Sheriff Bobby Craft in Vernon Parish and Sheriff Mitchell Newman in Cypress County, Texas. When she hung up, she reflected on what had gone wrong. Was it her fault, she wondered. How could a beautiful weekend go so horribly wrong? Elizabeth then sat in silence, all alone. She could hear every noise, every conversation. Her senses were so keen she could hear a ballpoint pen click down the hallway at the nurses' desk.

It wasn't long before Poppy and Kurt walked into the waiting room and sat beside her. Poppy never knew Elizabeth to be the emotional type, but today was the exception. She could barely speak, so Poppy just held her. A few people entered the waiting room, but they were all quiet. They were probably waiting for news of their loved one, too. Poppy glanced at Kurt, who had just returned to the waiting room after seeing a nurse he knew. He looked at Poppy and shook his head. Poppy knew what that meant and was glad Elizabeth had not seen him. Kurt then walked over to the couch and sat down next to them. No one said a word.

An hour had passed when the surgeon came into the room. He walked over and sat next to Elizabeth. She looked at him through tear-drenched, blood-shot eyes.
"Are you Elizabeth?" Dr. Delucia asked.
"Yes, I'm Elizabeth."
"Would you like to go in and see Jerry?"
Elizabeth nodded, and she stood up and followed the doctor. She paused for just a second and looked back at Poppy. Then she extended her hand to Poppy, who got up and joined her and the doctor as they approached Jerry's room. He was lying on his back with IVs in both arms. He looked up at

Elizabeth and smiled a weak smile. She took his hand and kissed his forehead. He smiled at her again, then shut his eyes for the last time. Still holding Jerry's hand, Elizabeth sat down hard on the chair beside Jerry's bed. She looked at Poppy.

"He's gone, Poppy. My Jerry is gone," Elizabeth said as tears filled her eyes.

Poppy was trying to hold her emotions in as best she could. She couldn't lose her composure—there was too much work to be done. Her feeling had now turned to anger. She would find Marley Powell if it were the last thing she did on this earth!

Sheriff Craft had sent Deputy Paul Yeary to investigate and assist Elizabeth. His assignment was to get as much information as possible from her while being supportive. Once he finished the interview at the hospital, he offered to take Elizabeth back home. It wasn't necessary because she had Poppy and Kurt to take care of her. And thankfully so, because Elizabeth needed a big shoulder to lean on.

Yeary returned to the Sheriff's office with a heavy heart. They all knew and worked with Jerry and respected him. The thought of him dying so needlessly hit home with all of the Sheriff's office employees. Sheriff Craft immediately contacted Sheriff Mitchell Newman in Texas to coordinate the investigation. After much discussion, they decided that Assistant District Attorney Poppy Nichols should head up a task force since she was also a sworn U.S. Deputy Marshal. They needed someone to work both sides of the Sabine River, and she fit the bill. The fact that she was close to Elizabeth and Jerry was something they took into consideration, but they still felt she was the best they had to take this on.

When Poppy got Elizabeth home, she helped her undress and settled her into a bathrobe. After pouring herself a glass of wine, she told Elizabeth she would take care of the notifications for her. Elizabeth was grateful. She didn't have it in her to talk to anyone right now. What happened today still seemed so surreal. Poppy placed a call to Elizabeth's mother and told her the sad news. After the shock wore off, Mrs. Weaver said she could be in Leesville within four hours. She would finally meet Elizabeth's mother, but this is not how she had planned it. Poppy ended the call and went to check on Elizabeth. The doctor at the hospital had given her a sedative, and it was no surprise that she was sleeping. Poppy left her tucked in and returned to the couch in the living room. She shut her eyes, but she was not sleeping. She was thinking about Marley Powell and how she was going to rein him in.

As Poppy shut her eyes, she played back this tragic day in her mind. In doing so, she remembered a doctor with a clipboard had stopped them as they left the hospital. Trying not to be insensitive, he told Elizabeth that he noticed her fiancé was an organ donor and asked her if she would be up to signing the necessary papers to complete the process. Elizabeth looked at him briefly and knew that time was of the essence to preserve the organs, so she accepted the offered document. She signed on all the required lines and handed it back to the doctor.

Sheriffs Craft and Newman met at the Vernon Parish Sheriff's office in Leesville to discuss how they would proceed with the investigation. The killing of an investigator was going to take priority over everything else. The decision was made to pull in all their deputies, whether from vacations or special assignments that weren't drug-related.

"Mitchell, I'm telling you that Marley Powell will be taken, and I don't care how. I don't give a damn if he's brought here in a body bag, but he will be taken," Sheriff Craft said.

"You got no argument from me, Bobby. This crap has gone on long enough. It ends now. A fly won't be able to get through Cypress County, Texas, without being stopped."

"The order I'll give my deputies will be to give him one chance to surrender. After that, well, it will be up to him if he lives or dies," Sheriff Craft said.

"Same here, Bobby. Glad to see we're on the same page."

Sheriff Craft knew Elizabeth would be out of the office for a while. He didn't want to interrupt her grieving process, but he had promised to keep her informed of events as they unfolded. He told her she could be part of the investigation whenever she felt up to it.

In the meantime, Poppy was glad that she was heading up the team that was looking into Jerry's murder. She had told Sheriff Bobby Craft that she was determined to find Marley Powell and whoever had killed James Lewis, even if it was on her own time. But Poppy was thinking to herself, was this revenge she was feeling? She realized no, this was not revenge. She looked at the plaque on her desk, a gift from Elizabeth when she was first hired.

Justice:
God demands it
Victims cry for it
We in LAW ENFORCEMENT deliver it

Poppy thought back to the days before her mother, Grace MacDonald, had adopted her before she had turned fourteen years old. She had been beaten, kidnapped, mistreated and neglected. Those horrible days when she felt there was no justice in the world. All those memories came flooding back. Unlike then, she was now grown, determined, and in a position to bring justice to the victim.

So, this was not revenge but justice—no matter how you bottled it, Poppy would deliver!

CHAPTER 26

A FAMILY MATTER

When Marley reached the Texas side of the lake, his arm was throbbing and stinging. He removed his coat, then his shirt, exposing one square inch of missing flesh and muscle. The right shoulder of his shirt was soaked in blood. Marley made his way to his car and found an old t-shirt that he tore into strips. He then wrapped his wound, sat in the seat behind the steering wheel, and cursed out loud.

Going to a hospital was not an option. Gunshot wounds were reported immediately. And, if he went to Nick's office, he would likely be killed by one of Nick's guys for taking the stolen coins and keeping the money for himself. He had no choice but to cross back to Louisiana by boat when it got dark. His family on that side of the lake would help him, as they always had. The thought of crossing Toledo Bend Lake with high winds, below-freezing temperatures, and at night was not for the faint of heart.

Marley knew that law enforcement on both sides of the Sabine would be looking for him. He also knew the shot he fired at Marshal Weaver hit Jerry Lambert. Marley had heard him groan and saw Lambert fall onto the boat's steering wheel. He wondered if the investigator was dead. If he was, then Marley had to get the hell out of the Texas/Louisiana area fast. From all his experience with law enforcement, he knew that killing one of them ramped up the manhunt. In other words, there would be no stopping them—they would look for him forever. He also figured that Marshal Weaver knew she had hit him with her pistol round. She might not know the extent of the wound, but she knew she had more than just clipped him. Stopping at a convenience store was out of the question with the way he was bleeding. Anyone looking at him would be able to tell he had been shot. All he could do now was wait for darkness to set in over the freezing, icy lake.

The cold wind off the lake hit his car head-on as it sat on a small knoll. Marley started the car and turned the heater on. He got the interior as hot as possible, then shut the engine off. He laid back in his seat, hoping to get some much-needed sleep. He woke up two hours later shivering. It was ice cold in the car, and his right arm was throbbing and painful. He looked down at his wound and saw that the makeshift bandage was soaked in blood. What now, he thought. It's still about four hours until darkness sets in. He got out of the car and walked to the shoreline, then looked across the lake toward Louisiana. The air and wind were biting cold. His face was numb, and his ears felt like someone was sticking needles in them. Navigating in twenty-eight degrees, with a twenty-mile-an-hour ice-cold blast of wind in choppy water, wasn't his preference, but it was the only way to get to the other side. Staring at the lake, he realized there were no boaters. Was this a good thing or a bad thing? It didn't matter—he had no choice. He had to risk it. It was either die here or possibly die on the lake. His mind made up, he pulled his boat into the water, got in, and hit the ignition. The motor groaned and turned over, sputtering. He revved the engine, pointed the boat into the east wind, and started for Louisiana.

The conditions were treacherous, and it took Marley over an hour and a half to get to the Louisiana side of the lake. At least he had made it, though. It wasn't any wonder no one else was out on the lake in this weather. As he moored the boat, he called his uncle, gave him his location, and asked him to come get him.

Marley waited in a wooded area on the north side of a campground until he saw the lights of his uncle's old pickup truck. Once inside the truck, he leaned back against the seat so weak he could barely speak. His Uncle Dave looked closely at the wound and told him he should see a doctor. He knew that Marley's wound did not look good. Not only had he been unable to stem the bleeding, but the area around it was inflamed. It was all Marley could do to shake his head in defiance. He was not going to a doctor or a hospital. He knew that would be a death sentence.

"How did you get shot?" His uncle asked.

"Marshal Weaver and Jerry Lambert came upon me in the lake when my motor stopped. Weaver recognized me, and before I could pick up my gun and aim, she fired at me, hitting me in the shoulder. I still got a shot off, but my aim wasn't the best, and I hit Lambert. I'm not sure where I struck him, and I'm not sure if he's dead or alive."

"You did what? You're an idiot! Don't you know every law enforcement officer in two states, plus the Feds, will be up in our woods? What you've done is led them right to us. You got to get the hell away from here. I can let you stay a few days at my house, but even then, I'm taking a big chance. If we weren't kin, I sure wouldn't be helping you. There's a remote cabin on Wolf Creek where you can stay while you mend. After that, you're on your own."

"Understood, Uncle Dave. I'll move on just as soon as I'm able."

Uncle Dave then filled him in on more trouble he had coming his way. "We had two guys show up at Butch's house yesterday looking for you. One said his name was Max Bren, and the other was a short, nasty fellow named Seaux. According to them, you ripped off a guy named Nick Durant, and he ain't too pleased. This Bren fellow said you stole gold coins worth a hundred thousand dollars. When they showed up, there were six of us at Butch's house. We thought with half a dozen of us there, they might be intimidated and back off. Boy, were we wrong. The Seaux guy said to tell you that if he had to come after you, he would slit your throat. He said you have until the end of the week to return the coins. Marley, he looked like the kind of guy who doesn't make empty threats. He told us we would be next if he didn't get the coins or the money. I got the impression he would enjoy killing all of us just for pleasure."

Marley sat back in the seat and took a deep breath. Everything was going wrong, he thought. My life has become a train wreck. Then, a burst of pain resonated through his shoulder. He winced and groaned as the pain reverberated through his entire body. What in the hell had he done to deserve this?

When Marley arrived at his uncle's home, his cousin was there. Not just any cousin—this one had been a medic in the Army. His uncle had called him on the way in and asked him to look at Marley's wound. After removing the makeshift bandage, he exposed a gaping hole.

"This is more than nasty. You should have had it looked at when it first happened," his cousin told him.

"I was a bit preoccupied at the time. Spare me your lecture, Abe, and tell me you can help me."

"Well, you're going to need some antibiotics. In fact, you should have already been on them cause in another eight hours, that wound will be septic."

Marley looked at him, unsure what septic meant, and asked. "So, let's say I go 'septic,' what happens then?"

"What happens is you die. I'll clean the wound the best I can. I have some antibiotics and a bottle of oxycodone at home I can give you. They're left over from a root canal I had last year. That may take the edge off the pain, but that's the best I can do for you, Marley. Without proper care, this just might kill you."

He nodded to let Abe know he understood.

Marley turned his attention to his Uncle Dave and asked him to come close to where he was lying. He told his uncle that he had a plan to get some pressure off himself. It involved ratting out James Lewis' killer. It was Nick Durant's man, someone he highly relied on and trusted. "You already met him. He's that Max Bren guy who came around looking for me. He accidentally killed James, but instead of reporting it, Nick told him to bury his body. You're gonna help me let that cat out of the bag. Hand me pen and paper."

Marley wrote down the details of the killing as he knew them and showed it to his Uncle Dave. He planned to give the note to his cousin Abe so he could make calls to Sheriffs Newman and Craft anonymously. Marley knew that the call about James Lewis' murder wouldn't get their total attention. But the location of the next heist planned by Nick Durant's men would, especially when it panned out. It was to take place at a pawn shop, and the haul included high-end jewelry and guns. They could catch Durant's guys in the act with the details given to them. And it would give them probable cause to interrogate Max Bren. Marley knew Max was physically strong, but he was mentally weak, and if any pressure were put on him, he would fold like a deck of cheap playing cards. He also knew that Bren had to be separated from Durant for questioning. Past experience told him that Max always looked at Durant for his approval before doing anything.

Abe had a friend who used burner phones in his line of work. He never asked his friend any questions—figured it was none of his business. But that friend could be helpful now, and he owed Abe a favor. Once Abe had acquired an untraceable phone, he would call Sheriff Newman first because the heist would be in his jurisdiction. His next call would be to Sheriff Craft to relay the same information and provide him with the name of James Lewis' killer. After all, the murder had occurred in his jurisdiction.

CHAPTER 27

RAID IN CYPRESS COUNTY

Sheriff Mitchell Newman was leaving his office at the end of a day shift when his phone rang. He hesitated for a minute and then decided to pick up. When the caller asked if he was Sheriff Newman, he answered, "Affirmative."

"Well, Sheriff, I have some information for you regarding an upcoming burglary that will take place in your county," the caller said.

Newman couldn't help but wonder if this was a hoax. Typically, he was notified about a crime after it happened unless rival criminal factions were trying to throw each other under the bus. "Can I ask why you want to report this? What's in it for you?" Newman asked.

"Look, do you want the information or not?" The caller asked.

"Sure, give me the details," the Sheriff said as he grabbed a pen and a piece of paper.

The caller provided details about a pawn shop heist that hadn't taken place yet. But what he said before he hung up got Newman's attention.

"I also know who killed James Lewis, and the same people are involved."

Newman wondered if he had heard him correctly. "Son, how do you know this?" All he got in response was a click on the other end of the line. The caller had hung up.

Abe's next phone call was to Sheriff Craft in Vernon Parish. Craft was completing some paperwork when the dispatcher called him on the intercom.

"Sheriff, there's a guy on the phone who says he knows who killed James Lewis."

Hopefully, this was a good lead and not some prankster. "Go ahead and put him through on my private line," the Sheriff told her.

When Craft answered the phone, he asked the caller to identify himself.

"That's a firm no, sir. Look, I have details of James Lewis' murder. Do you want the info or not?"

231

The Sheriff told him yes, and Abe proceeded to tell him what had led up to the killing and who was involved.

When Abe mentioned Nick Durant's name, Sheriff Craft said nothing; he just listened. The name was familiar to him as a shady character who operated primarily in Texas. They'd never been able to put their hands on him. He was suspected of illegal activity, mainly dealing in stolen goods, but they never had enough evidence to arrest him.

The Sheriff interrupted him and asked, "What's the connection between this Nick Durant and James Lewis?"

The caller explained that James Lewis was fencing property for Durant. He no longer wanted to be a part of a criminal element. James was very good at unloading the stolen merchandise, so Durant didn't want to lose him. He sent his right-hand man, Max Bren, to find James and intimidate him into staying with their enterprise.

The Sheriff jumped in again and asked, "How did intimidation turn into murder? Killing James Lewis wouldn't further Durant's business."

Abe told him that it was an accident. Lewis wasn't supposed to get hurt. When Bren found Lewis on the river, he was pulling sinker logs. Bren paddled up, intending to talk to him, but an argument ensued. He hit Lewis over the head with a heavy boat paddle. The blow to Lewis' head was only supposed to get his attention. But Bren, being a big guy, had put too much weight into the swing. Once he realized that Lewis was dead, he panicked and called Nick Durant. At first, Durant was pissed—he didn't want James killed. He was his biggest fencer. But then he saw a way to salvage what had happened and use it to his advantage. He instructed Bren to bury James Lewis in a shallow grave on the Major's property. He knew that Lewis' body would eventually be found, and it would add fuel to an already simmering feud.

As soon as Sheriff Craft hung up, a deputy standing in his office doorway advised him that Sheriff Mitchell Newman urgently needed to speak to him. After comparing notes, the Sheriffs wasted no time formulating a plan to stop Nick Durant's criminal activity and to put Max Bren behind bars where he belonged.

The caller had indicated that the burglary would take place in two nights, so there was no time to be wasted. The team was quickly assembled for a meeting at the Cypress County Sheriff's office. District Attorney O'Connor gladly agreed to allow Poppy to participate. It was late in the evening when they sat down in the conference room to discuss the information given by the anonymous caller.

The crime was to be committed at the *Highway 63 Pawn Shop*. The plan included short-circuiting the alarm system at both entrances of the building. Once inside, two safes needed to be opened. One was where the 'valuable' goods, such as jewelry and coins, were kept—the second safe stored firearms. The caller's information was that a plasma torch was to be used on each safe. There would be four participants, including Max Bren, who would be the lookout and the driver. The other three would be inside, gaining access to the two safes. Nick Durant would stay behind at his office waiting to inventory the night's take. The action was scheduled to begin at one o'clock in the morning. Sheriffs Craft and Newman advised the team that they had no way to verify the informant's tip, but after much discussion, they decided the information was too detailed to ignore. Each team member was given their assignment beforehand so they would be ready for the raid. They weren't leaving anything to chance.

They started preparing at 10:00 p.m. on the night of the break-in by meeting at the Cypress County Sheriff's office. Sheriffs Newman and Craft had put together a select team to be a part of the take-down. Poppy was appointed as a team lead and wasted no time selecting a few deputies from both departments to stay back and keep a close eye on Nick Durant's office in Bon Wier, Texas. Just in case he got knowledge of the raid and tried to run like a rat abandoning a ship.

The deputies kept a diligent watch and were rewarded when, at 1:00 a.m., a large Ford pickup truck drove around to the rear of the pawnshop. One man got out and cut the power to the building. Two more went to the large steel door at the back and cut the locking mechanism with a torch. When the door opened, with precision timing, three of the individuals went inside the business and immediately started burning the safes. After seeing them enter, two of Sheriff Newman's deputies ran to the pickup truck and grabbed Max Bren. They threw a dark bag over his head and then handcuffed him. He was dragged to a Sheriff's SUV and strapped in tightly. Bren's first thought was that Nick was going to have him killed for his screw-up with James Lewis. Then he heard a police radio. He never thought he'd be happy to hear that squawking. He breathed a sigh of relief and sat in the SUV with his head down, remaining silent.

Four deputies entered the pawnshop, walked quietly up behind the men working on the safe, and pointed guns at their heads. Then, all the deputies' lights came on, and the men stopped what they were doing and raised their hands. The men were separated and briefly questioned. After they admitted they worked for Nick Durant, they were brought to Sheriff Mitchell Newman's holding cells. The team watching Durant's office was given the 'go-ahead'.

The raid at Nick Durant's office didn't go as easily. The deputies announced they had a warrant and immediately battered the door. Some of Durant's people decided to shoot it out. One of them was Durant's enforcer, Pete Seaux, who was in the conference room when the raid began. Two of his other associates had been walking down the hall and were in the direct line of fire from the entry door. They pulled their guns and started firing randomly. The deputies returned fire, hitting all of them. All three men fell, including Seaux, who was climbing out a window and firing at the same time. Nick came out of his office with his hands in the air along with two other associates. Durant was smart—he'd rather fight it out in court than get gunned down in a hallway like his associates. He was separated from the others and transported to a holding cell at Sheriff Mitchell Newman's office. They knew there was no sense questioning Durant. He would let his lawyer do the talking.

Max Bren was brought into the interview room by two deputies. They sat him down and handcuffed him to the interview table. Poppy watched him for a while through a window. He appeared nervous, which was to be expected. The deputy standing next to Poppy asked if she wanted him with her in the interview room.

She looked at him, shook her head, and said, "I've got this." Poppy turned, opened the door, and walked into the room.

She sat and looked at him, remaining silent for a minute. At first, he wouldn't make eye contact with her. She kept staring at him until he looked up. Bren was a big guy, but Poppy noticed he had the mannerisms of a child. She decided to change her interview technique with him. She could tell that a high-pressure approach would not garner much. The softer technique seemed the right way to go. She started by asking him his name.

In a soft voice, he answered her. "It's Max."

"Are you hungry, Max?" She asked.

He nodded and looked at her with a smile.

Poppy walked to the door and asked the deputy to bring him some potato chips, a candy bar, and a soft drink. They brought them in and handed the snacks to Max. He opened them and ate.

While eating, Poppy asked him how long he had known Nick Durant. His answer was 'a long time'. She stopped the interview and gave him his rights. She asked if he understood what she was saying. He nodded. Poppy asked him to provide a verbal answer.

"Yes, I understand."

"Do you have any knowledge of the death of James Lewis, Max?"

"Yes, I do," Max answered.

"Does that mean you know who killed him?" Poppy asked.

"Well, yes. I did, but it was an accident. Nick said to scare him and maybe rough him up a little, but I didn't mean to kill him." Max lowered his head and quit eating. "I never wanted to hurt anybody. I liked James. He would always bring me licorice 'cause he knew I liked it. I really miss James."

Poppy paused for a minute. She empathized with Max. Nick Durant manipulated and used him, knowing he was mentally slow. There was no doubt Max would not have hurt James Lewis on purpose. This made Poppy angry. The evil that was in Nick Durant was disgusting. But she still had a job, and more questions had to be asked. The only difference this time was the soft tone of her voice.

"Did you bury him on the McKay property?" Poppy asked.

"Yes, I did what Nick told me to do. I called Nick and told him what happened, and he laughed and told me to bury him on the Major's property in a shallow grave so someone could find him. He said they would think the Major did it, which would keep that feud going. He thought that was hilarious."

"Did you think it was funny, Max?"

"No, hurting someone is not funny."

"Max, can I ask you why you did it then?"

"Because I work for Nick, and he told me to."

Poppy stayed calm, but she was boiling mad inside. "Okay, Max, thank you. That's all I need from you right now." She motioned for the deputy to come in and take Max to his cell.

Max looked up at her and smiled.

When she walked out of the interview room, both Sheriffs were there and had listened to the entire interview. When they saw the look on Poppy's face, they knew exactly what she was thinking. Nick Durant was in for one hell of a tongue-lashing.

Poppy went into the Sheriff's breakroom and poured herself a cup of coffee. As she sat down, Sheriff Newman pulled up a chair.

She looked at Mitchell with a stern and determined look. "Mitchell, I'm going to finish this coffee, take some deep breaths, then go to the interview room. If Nick Durant will talk to me, I will rip him a new one."

"Take him to the cleaners, Poppy," Mitchell told her.

It was thirty minutes before they brought Durant into the interview room. Once inside, he was cuffed to the table. Poppy gave him ten minutes to stew; then she walked in.

"I'm Poppy Nichols, Assistant District Attorney for Vernon Parish, Louisiana. I'm also a sworn United States Marshall. You are being charged with state and federal crimes in Texas and Louisiana. These charges include fifteen counts of grand theft, twenty counts of burglary, racketeering, and conspiracy to commit murder. I understand you've been read your rights. Do you have anything to say?"

"Yes, I want an attorney," Durant said.

"That's fine. I'm glad you're keeping your mouth shut. That means no reduction in your sentence for cooperating. You're looking at one hundred and fifty years in prison, scumbag." She turned and walked out of the room, seething but confident in her ability to put Nick Durant behind bars for a long time.

CHAPTER 28

PEACE ON THE SABINE?

Twenty-four hours after Poppy interviewed Max Bren, she and Sheriff Mitchell Newman drove out to Rufus Lewis' home. They felt he'd waited long enough to find out who had made sure his son no longer walked this earth. No sense putting it off any longer. He had a right to know. They hadn't called him to let him know they were coming. The news they had was best delivered in person.

It was late morning, and Rufus was just getting home from his sawmill down the road. The late winter weather still carried a chill in the air. As Poppy exited Mitchell's SUV, that chill penetrated her clothing and went straight to her core. She shivered slightly as she looked at Rufus standing on the front porch. As they approached, they heard a loud squawking sound coming from overhead. They looked up at the cloudless sky and saw a determined hawk circling.

"That bastard is looking for one of my chickens," Rufus said, pointing to the hawk.

They smiled as they walked onto the porch.

"Rufus, we have news for you. The murderer of your son has been arrested," Poppy said.

Rufus was silent for a minute as he studied their faces. When he'd seen them drive up, he thought it was to deliver more excuses as to why they hadn't caught James' killer yet. He didn't expect this news—it plainly shocked him. When he finally spoke, he asked if they were sure. Yes, they told him. The killer had actually confessed and provided details.

"Who did it?" Rufus asked angrily. "Was it one of the McKays?"

Poppy told him no, then went into detail about who committed the act and how it came to be. It was no consolation to Rufus that James' killer had only meant to scare him. At the end of the day, he was still dead and buried in the cold ground.

When Poppy finished her explanation, Rufus wanted Durant and wanted him dead. He knew Durant from the time his sons were in high school with him. In fact, he and James were pretty close back then. Rufus didn't know that friendship had continued after high school and sports. And he certainly didn't know that James was fencing stolen property for Durant. But Rufus was relieved to find out that because of Bonnie Blue, he wanted out of the business. He heard rustling behind him and turned to see his wife standing in the doorway. She had tears seeping from her eyes. She had been listening to the entire conversation. She was primarily a quiet woman, keeping her thoughts to herself and rarely speaking when Poppy visited. But today, things were gonna change. She had stayed silent too long.

Norma stepped out onto the porch and said her piece. She was addressing everyone, but make no mistake, the message was mostly for her husband.

"This ridiculous, childish feud has gone on long enough. It never was the McKay's doing. It wasn't entirely your fault either, Rufus. But just the same both families suffered because of it. Bonnie Blue was a ray of light for James. She was turning him around. You're a fool if you don't see that. If this feud continues, I don't want it to be because of us. It stops here today. Do you understand Rufus? Today!"

Rufus looked at her, almost sheepishly, and nodded. He knew she was right, and he would make the peace offering. When folks on the Sabine River gave their word and shook hands, it was a bond, a contract, a sacred trust. Rufus intended to go to the Major's and offer an apology.

The chill that Poppy had felt upon her arrival at the Lewis' was gone. Oh, the winter weather was still there, but she felt warm inside and out. Mitchell looked at her and asked if she was ready to leave. Poppy smiled and nodded. After all the turmoil that had gone on, it was finally over. They started walking back to Mitchell's SUV. Poppy paused for a second and turned to look at the Lewises standing on the porch. She saw Rufus Lewis smile and wave for the first time. She smiled and waved back. They climbed into the SUV and left.

Rufus glanced down at his wife and told her he was going across the river to see if the Major was home. There was a lot to be said, and he was ready to end this feud. He hoped the Major would accept his apology, but if he didn't, as far as Rufus was concerned, the feud had ended. If the Major wanted to continue it, he could feud with himself!

It was early afternoon when Rufus pulled his old pickup into the Major's driveway. He parked by the large fountain in front of the house. Before proceeding to the front door, he turned and looked at his beat-up truck sitting next to the three-tiered fountain out front. It sure looked out of place. He was referring to his truck and not the fountain. Major always had been fond of the fancy stuff. For the first time in years, Rufus wasn't carrying his pistol. He had hung it up. He was tired of conflict, and besides, the large frame .44 magnum was an intimidator. The years of bad blood and disputes had taken a toll on him and his family. Today, hopefully, this would come to an end for him and the McKays.

As he approached the veranda, the Major stepped out of his front door. Rufus walked straight up to him and extended his hand. The Major responded by clasping Rufus' hand snuggly.

The Major had already received a call from Poppy advising him what had transpired in Durant's office in Bon Wier, Texas, yesterday and about today's visit with the Lewises. The Major had done a lot of thinking since that phone call and realized there was no reason to carry on the feud. It was senseless, and both families had suffered because of it. He had planned to go to the Lewis home that afternoon to see if they could make amends.

Rufus was the first to speak and offered a sincere apology to the Major. The Major responded in kind and invited him inside. They spoke about topics that should have been discussed years ago and came up with solutions they could both live with. A gentleman's agreement was reached with respect to the logs and a few other things that had caused consternation in the past. Consternation to them and their ancestors before them that carried this feud on for over a hundred years. All those years of fighting had been put to rest in a brief period.

As Rufus left, he stopped on the veranda and asked the Major if he could speak briefly with Bonnie Blue. The Major nodded and turned to walk into the house.

Soon, Bonnie Blue came through the doorway.

"Bonnie, my wife, and I were going through James' room after his death and found this." Rufus handed her a gift-wrapped box. "There was also a card attached to it with your name on it. We didn't open either."

Bonnie thanked him and took the card and small package from Rufus' hand. She opened the box first. Inside, on a satin bed, lay a white gold star of Sirius with a sapphire stone set in the middle. She opened the card and read it to herself first. She knew Rufus wanted to know one of the last things James had written, and she wanted to share those words with him. So, she read:

"For my beautiful Bonnie Blue. May your love shine as bright as the brightest star in the heavens.
All My Love Forever,
Your James"

Bonnie looked up at Rufus with tears trickling down her cheeks. He smiled and thanked her, and then Rufus reached out with his big, calloused hand. She extended hers, and he took it and squeezed it softly. He turned and started walking to his truck.

"Mr. Lewis, will you wait a minute?" Bonnie asked.

Rufus stopped and turned to see Bonnie run toward him. When she got close, she wrapped her arms around his neck and kissed him on the cheek.

Rufus smiled, looked down at her, and said, "Thank you, Bonnie."

She stood in the driveway and watched Rufus climb into his truck. She looked down sadly at the star necklace and the note, clutched them in her hand, and walked back into the house. She was thankful to have James' last gift to her. She just hadn't decided if the true gift was the star of Sirius or the end of the feud. There was one thing she was sure of. The Lewises were good people, and now all the McKays knew it. After dealing with the tragedy of James' death, this made her very happy. As happy as she had been in a long time.

CHAPTER 29

HOW DO I SAY GOODBYE?

    Elizabeth couldn't help replaying the scene in her head over and over again even though Jerry's fatal shooting by Marley Powell took place four days ago. She remembered hearing the gunshots and seeing her fiancé slumping over onto the boat steering wheel. Then her desperation as she rushed him to the landing to meet the EMS personnel. She couldn't forget the smile that he gave her as they loaded him into the ambulance. And she could still hear his labored breathing as the paramedics worked on him. As she re-lived the moment that she gazed into his dying eyes, even the morning sun on her face couldn't warm the chill that had engulfed her. Elizabeth's world had fallen apart.

Elizabeth and Poppy arrived at the Parish Funeral Home around mid-morning. Jerry had no living relatives, so she was the only one who could instruct the funeral director about the arrangements. At least, that's what she thought. As if handling everything herself might change what had transpired. What if they hadn't been on the lake that day? They had taken the day off from fishing and enjoyed each other's company at the cabin. What if she had gotten off the first shot and taken Marley down? She knew she was the one who had to do this. She felt she owed it to Jerry, maybe as some penance for what she had allowed to happen to him. She couldn't get it out of her head that it was all her fault and wished she could go back and change that day's events.

Elizabeth sat down with the funeral director, who, with much serenity, presented several choices for her selection. Poppy was by her side and saw that she struggled to get through this meeting. How could she be expected to pick out a casket, the color of the lining, flowers, music, and everything else that he was going on and on about? Didn't this man realize she had just lost her soulmate? Poppy saw the expression on Elizabeth's face, so she was not surprised when she broke down in the middle of the meeting, stood up, and said she just couldn't finish. Not today, and maybe not another day. She stood up and went out into the hallway. Poppy told the director she would be right back, and then she followed her out the door.

Elizabeth was leaning against the wall and heard someone come up behind her. She turned and saw it was Poppy. "I feel his arms around me when I walk, sit, or lay down. I smell his scent everywhere. I thought I saw him walking down Third Street just yesterday. Poppy, my heart is breaking, and I don't know how to fix it."

Poppy's heart sank as she held Elizabeth. She let her get all the tears out as she wept. She could feel her trembling. She knew that even though Elizabeth was mentally strong, this was one task she could not handle. Poppy pulled away from her and looked her in the eyes.

"Let me finish making the arrangements for you. I know your wishes and will ensure they are carried out just as if you had done it yourself. Is that okay?"

Elizabeth nodded, and Poppy guided her to a couch in the sitting room to wait while she went back to finish the meeting with the director. Poppy had already pictured how this day would go in her mind and had been prepared to step in.

She returned to the funeral director's office, and he asked if Ms. Weaver was okay. "No, she's not, but she will be. I'll be handling the details for her."

After planning the final arrangements at the funeral home, Poppy contacted Pastor Eddie Tilley at his Community

Church and asked him to officiate at Jerry's service. He had been expecting the call and gladly accepted, telling her he was honored to give Investigator Lambert the proper sendoff for his meeting with his Maker. She told him what arrangements she had made at the Parish Funeral Home, and Pastor Tilley volunteered to coordinate the church service with them. She graciously accepted, thankful this day was almost over but knowing the most challenging day was still to come. Poppy had to be strong because it was up to her to help Elizabeth get through it.

On a cold and breezy winter day, friends started arriving at Pastor Tilley's church in the Burr Ferry community. First to arrive were Elizabeth, Poppy, and Kurt, and they took their seats in the front pew. After a few minutes, Elizabeth leaned over, choking back tears, and whispered to Poppy.

"I call Jerry's cell phone daily just to hear his voice. Two days before he died, I told him we were perfect together. You know what he told me, Poppy?"

Looking at Elizabeth, Poppy shook her head.

"He told me we were *beautifully flawed.*" She said with a smile. "*Beautifully flawed,* Poppy. How poetic and accurate. I never thought I would lose him. I'm broken, Poppy, I'm so broken," Elizabeth said, looking at Poppy with tears on her cheeks and a heartbreaking sadness in her eyes. Poppy could not find the words to ease Elizabeth's sorrow. She put her arms around her shoulders and held her while she wept. For a moment, Poppy could see what Elizabeth saw and feel what she felt. It was like Elizabeth's heart was breaking inside her.

When the time came for the service to start, Pastor Tilley walked up to the pulpit, paused, and looked around at the overflow of people in the church. Behind Elizabeth's pew sat Sheriffs Craft and Newman. He could see the sad but determined look on their faces. Seated in the middle of the church were the Lewises and the McKays—all of them, including their sons and daughters, with their respective families. And for the first time, they were seated on the same side of the church.

Rufus was looking straight ahead, displaying a stoic look. He was showing a sadness no one had seen from him since his son, James, went missing. He hardly blinked his eyes as he sat there. Then he bowed his head as if in silent prayer. Rufus' wife, Norma, took his hand and squeezed it.

The Major stared out of the church's western window as if deep in thought. After several minutes of gazing, he straightened up and looked at the floor between his feet. Margo put her hand on his shoulder and rubbed him gently on the back. She whispered something in his ear, and the Major stood up and turned around to face Rufus, who was seated behind him. The Major reached out his hand to Rufus, who shook it firmly—their display of friendship broadcast to the community that the feud was over. There had been rumors that the Lewis and McKays had reached an agreement and put their dispute to rest. Now, the patriarchs had just confirmed it. There were low whispers in the church as the Pastor opened his bible to signal that the service was about to begin. Suddenly, there was nothing but silence.

Before Pastor Tilley began, he thought back to when Elizabeth and Jerry came to him with their wedding plans. He knew that this was in God's plan, but why this beautiful God-fearing couple, who were starting their lives together? Only God knew the answer. Pastor Tilley had no vengeance in his heart, but he prayed that Jerry's murderer would soon be caught and dealt with.

He looked at Elizabeth and smiled. In a low voice, he said, "We will help you get through this."

With tears running down her cheeks, she smiled back at him and nodded. Pastor Tilley then looked at the people in the congregation who were paying their last respects to Jerry. He remained silent for a moment as he surveyed the attendees. He took a deep breath and looked at Beverly, his wife. She knew this was going to be hard on him. She nodded as if to say you can do this, Eddie, he smiled at her and then began to speak.

"God gives His strongest soldiers His toughest battles," Pastor Tilley paused and looked down. He pulled a handkerchief from his suit pocket and wiped his eyes. He took another breath and looked up, then peered out at the congregation and spoke again.

"To each of you, I'm sorry for your loss. You knew Jerry differently, depending on how your paths crossed. And he was special to every one of you. Jerry and Elizabeth are two of God's powerful soldiers. As most of you know, Jerry attended church here. He had no living relatives. The closest person he had to family was his loving fiancé, Elizabeth Weaver. The love those two shared was timeless. You, each one of you, were also his family. His death was tragic, but his life was exemplary and should be an example for each of us. Jerry's eyes are still seeing, and his heart is still loving. The love he had for each of you can't be measured. He will be missed. But God had a divine plan for Jerry as He has for all of us. We don't always know or understand His Plan, but whatever it is, His Plan is perfect. I will leave you with this thought. I was talking with Jerry recently and asked him what his secret was to staying so positive and upbeat. He told me, 'I make the choice to love every day. We need to hold each other closer and a little more.' Wow, what an attitude; did you hear that? He chose *to love.* Those were Jerry's words. They should be our words also. What a way to live! Jerry spoke from the heart. That's what he did. That's what we all should do. I've never heard anyone say, 'I spent too much time loving someone.' Choose to love every day. Now, please bow your heads and let us all pray."

    As the service ended, the attendees slowly left the church. Although it was a powerful eulogy, few understood Pastor Tilley's words about God's divine plan. But they believed in the Pastor and his message. Soon, they would discover God's divine plan and how accurate Pastor Tilley's message was.

CHAPTER 30

WOLF CREEK

Marley's family helped get him moved to the cabin on Wolf Creek right after Abe created a distraction for the Sheriffs of Vernon Parish, Louisiana, and Cypress County, Texas. If they hadn't taken turns nursing him, he probably would be dead and buried by now. That didn't mean he was out of danger, though—just the threat of dying. He was a wanted man, and his entire family was aware of that fact and was adversely affected by it. Killing an individual, especially someone from the law enforcement community, brought its own special hell for the killer. And in this case, for the killer's family. Sheriff Craft and his deputies from Vernon Parish had been turning over every rock, looking for Marley. When locating him proved unsuccessful, they decided to turn up the heat on his family. And they felt that heat just as Sheriff Craft had intended. The Powells had their own illegal operations, which didn't include killing law enforcement officers. Because of the manhunt for Marley, they had almost shut down their moonshine operation, except for selling to the locals they'd known since the cradle. And it put a massive dent in their ability to fence stolen property. No one would deal with them—too afraid they would get caught up in the net. Two of Marley's cousins and an uncle had already been arrested for charges that would have been overlooked or given a warning in the past.

    The Powell family was ready for Marley to move on, but he seemed quite content hiding out in the cabin they had provided. After all, he had some money and was safe right where he was. He certainly had no plans to leave. Not with every law enforcement officer in two states looking for him. The Powells decided it was time to call all its members together for a meeting. Everyone that is except Marley.
    The discussion centered on how to bring their income levels back to where they were before Marley dragged them into his mess. Unsurprisingly, they agreed the only avenue going forward included getting rid of Marley. Or at least getting law enforcement to look for him someplace else. They floated around several ideas, but the popular one was telling him to leave. The only problem with that was there needed to be volunteers for the job! Marley was known for his bad temper and surly disposition. Which is how he got himself into the fix

he is in now. Another idea involved moving him to another location, preferably in another state! Again, there were no volunteers. One cousin pointed out that it wouldn't work because a deputy followed them almost every time one of them left home. Something had to be done, so they settled on what they believed was the best solution. Someone needed to turn him in anonymously, of course. They justified their decision by agreeing that if he were to go on the run, he would probably die in a gunfight. This way, he would get his day in court, and once convicted, he would get his three squares a day. No one wanted to be the rat, so they agreed they would draw numbers, and whoever got the number five would be the one to call. Of course, they wouldn't need to tell the others it was them. Just as long as it got done. Abe listened to all the back and forth but didn't speak up. He hadn't saved Marley's life, only for them to throw it away. Besides killing a law enforcement officer? Not only would Marley do hard time, but at the end of that time there would be a gas chamber waiting for him. His crime was punishable by death. Abe got in his car and left as soon as the meeting ended. Careful that he wasn't being followed, he made his way to the cabin on Wolf Creek. He had decided that his only choice was to warn Marley.

Things didn't go the way Abe thought they would. When he pulled up to the cabin, his cousin Marley was sitting on the front porch leisurely drinking a beer. To see him, you would think he didn't have a care in the world. Abe knew to tread lightly with him. He eased into the conversation by telling

Marley that he felt it was no longer safe for him there and that it was best if he left. Abe was emphatic when he told him he was concerned that if he were arrested, he would more than likely get a death sentence if he were found guilty. And he pointed out that Marley had plenty of money and could relocate wherever he wanted. He didn't need to stay in the immediate area. But Marley would have none of it. He was comfortable in the cabin, with law enforcement none the wiser about his location. That's when Abe dropped the bombshell and told him that a meeting had been called and a family member, he didn't know who, had been picked to turn him in. He thought this would be a huge incentive to leave. But the information only angered him more. He jumped up, threw the beer can to the ground, and ordered Abe to leave. He had no choice but to get in his car and go back the way he had come.

Marley was livid! He wasted no time calling a family meeting of his own via his Uncle Dave since he couldn't exactly leave the cabin. He had Dave deliver a message to each member of the family who participated in the earlier decision to turn him in. The message was, *"I will come for you when you least expect it—I will circle your house waiting for you to nod off—so sleep with one eye open for the rest of your life."* And, of course, he let Uncle Dave know that Abe had tipped him off.

Abe was now *persona non grata* with the entire family. All he had tried to do was to save his cousin Marley from what he was sure would be a certain death, and this is how he repaid him. He thought about how to get back into his family's good graces, and only one option floated to the top. He would put his plan into action the following morning.

Early the next day, Abe went to the Vernon Parish Sheriff's office. There was nothing anonymous about it. When he arrived, Deputy Paul Yeary was working the front desk. Abe reluctantly walked up to him and told him who he was and that he wanted to turn in his cousin for his own good. In return, he asked that they do their best not to hurt him. He admitted that Marley was heavily armed and would want to put up a fight. Yeary assured him that Sheriff Craft could handle the situation and would take all necessary precautions. With that promise received, he proceeded to give details on Marley Powell's location.

According to Abe, Marley was hiding in a remote cabin on Wolf Creek, approximately two hundred yards from Toledo Bend Lake. He had a boat stashed away in a cove there. Abe had even drawn a crude map to guide them. The cabin could be easily missed if you weren't familiar with the area. He filled Yeary in on Marley's wound, the severity of it, and the fact that it was pretty much healed. It wouldn't hamper him much. Just so they knew. Abe was reluctant to leave. What had he done? Was this a mistake? Had he, a Powell, just turned in his own cousin?

As soon as Abe left the station, Yeary called the Sheriff with details of his conversation with Abe Powell. The plan had worked. The Sheriff had put so much pressure on the Powells that they cracked and informed on Marley.

Elizabeth had been back at work for a week when she received an urgent call from Sheriff Craft.

"Elizabeth, we've received information from a reliable source on the whereabouts of Marley Powell. One of his relatives actually came to our office and told us that Marley was held up at a cabin on Wolf Creek. He even drew us a map. I wanted to give you the first crack. Do you want to be involved in his apprehension?"

"Absolutely, you know I do. Just tell me when and where, and I will be there, Bobby."

"So that you know, we will give him every opportunity to surrender, but we will be prepared for anything that presents itself," Sheriff Craft said.

Elizabeth knew that apprehending Marley wouldn't bring Jerry back. But it would be the start she needed to get on with her life. She also knew that if Marley didn't surrender, he would be coming out of that cabin feet first.

Sheriff Craft coordinated the operation with Sheriff Newman. Craft's people were to make entry at the cabin. Sheriff Newman would be on the lake with his deputies surrounding the cove in boats just in case he escaped toward the lake.

Newman's deputies had found Marley's boat, disabled the motor, and chopped a hole in the bottom of the craft. The sun was coming up and peeking through the clouds, distributing soft rays over the canopied forest of evergreens along Wolf Creek. As the deputies surrounded the cabin, they felt the chilly wintery wind coming off the lake. The chill these deputies felt wasn't just the winter wind but the evil emanating from the cabin on Wolf Creek. The lawmen were determined that no matter the situation, they would not leave until Powell came out of the cabin dead or alive. It didn't matter to them, but Powell would be coming out. Each time a deputy got into position, he acknowledged he was ready. Ten minutes later, Sheriff Newman called Sheriff Craft and told him his deputies were in position. Elizabeth was next to Sheriff Craft behind a pile of logs two hundred feet in front of the cabin. After ensuring everyone was set, he got out his bullhorn and turned it up as loud as possible.

"Marley Powell, this is Sheriff Bobby Craft. We have active warrants for you on murder, grand theft, interstate flight, felon in possession of a firearm, and racketeering. Walk through the front door, unarmed, with your fingers interlaced behind your head. This is your chance to surrender. DO IT NOW!"

Two minutes went by with no response. A shot rang out before Craft could pull the bullhorn back up to his mouth. A bullet from the cabin struck a tree, causing the bark to fly off five feet from where Craft was standing. He immediately got on the radio and gave the order to fire on the cabin. Elizabeth, who was standing next to Craft, grabbed an AR15 rifle and started emptying a clip of rounds into the cabin. The firing kept up for a few minutes before the front door of the cabin swung open, and two handguns and a rifle came flying out. Craft ordered a cease-fire. This was followed by Marley coming out, waving a white pillowcase in his right hand. Three deputies came running from the woods, threw Marley down on the ground face first, then searched and handcuffed him.

Marley started screaming that the handcuffs were too tight. They ignored his plea, and he uttered a new one. "I don't want to die!" No one was listening to him. He opened his eyes and looked to his left as he still lay face down. He saw a pair of women's shoes only inches from his face. He then looked up into the bright morning sun and saw the silhouetted body of a woman. Then he heard her speak.

"Got you, you bastard! It would be best if you had shot it out with us. Now, you are going to anticipate death every day of your short life. I will be there when you get the needle." Then she turned and walked away.

Marley started crying as he lay face down in the dirt. He knew it was too late for tears. His fate had been sealed just as he had sealed Jerry's fate.

Elizabeth had not had many good days since Jerry had died, but today was one of her better days. Not only because Marley Powell had been arrested and would pay for what he had done to Jerry, but she had gotten a surprise yesterday that lit up her world. She had tears of joy streaming down her cheeks as she got in her car and speed-dialed Poppy.

"Poppy, it's done. Powell is in custody. I can't tell you the weight that has been lifted from me. We need to talk. I have something very important to tell you. Can you get away?"
"Of course, I can. Where do you want to meet?" Poppy asked.

CHAPTER 31

LIFE AFTER DEATH

Poppy sat silently in the park as she waited for Elizabeth to arrive. She was a bundle of nerves, wondering what she wanted to tell her. Elizabeth had already told her on the phone that Marley Powell was in custody, but she didn't have to. It was the buzz at the office. The next step would be going to trial, but that was down the road, so that couldn't be it. Maybe Elizabeth has decided to leave Vernon Parish—too many memories? She had to tell herself to stop. She was getting all melancholy for no reason. She would be patient a little bit longer, just until Elizabeth arrived.

Elizabeth slowed as she approached the entrance to Vernon Parish Municipal Park. She made the turn and continued driving a quarter mile down the road until she stopped by an ancient oak tree whose limbs hovered over a weather-faded picnic table. The winter had stripped the old oak of its leaves, and the chill in the air was a stark reminder that winter was still here. The chill on her face was unpleasant as she exited the car. She saw Poppy sitting at the table, waiting for her.

Poppy looked up and saw her approach but couldn't read her facial expression. It wouldn't be long before she knew what Elizabeth wanted to impart to her. When Poppy was a child, she would shut her eyes tight and wish as hard as she could for something she wanted badly. The wishes weren't for material things. Her wishes were more about having a family to love her. She had to reach the ripe old age of thirteen before that wish came true. She realized that she had been sitting there with her eyes pressed tightly shut, praying that Elizabeth wasn't coming to tell her that she was going to leave in search of a place without the unwelcome memories.

Elizabeth hugged Poppy and took a seat next to her. She placed her oversized purse on top of the table and then reached inside. Poppy was surprised to see her pull out a thermos, which she set on the table. As she loosened the top, the aroma of hot cocoa filled the air. Elizabeth reached back into her bag and took out a split of champagne. Poppy watched her, transfixed on the combination of hot cocoa and champagne.

Elizabeth saw the curious expression on Poppy's face and decided not to keep her in suspense any longer. She slowly looked around and then up to the sky and smiled as her long blond hair cascaded down her back, and her deep blue eyes seemed to sparkle. She took a deep breath of the cold air and let it out slowly.

"I guess you are wondering why I brought you out here, right?"

"You could say that," Poppy said, fearing the worst.

"Well, this was mine and Jerry's spot. This was the first place we kissed." Elizabeth looked directly at Poppy with the glow still engulfing her face. "You know, I can still see him sitting right where you are, laughing at my silly jokes. I could tell him the corniest jokes just to hear him groan. We would talk about the future, the fun, and the challenges ahead of us. We grieve because Jerry's gone from us. God sees things from His perspective, not ours. You know what they say. When God closes one door, He opens another. He has opened another door for me, Poppy. I guess you can say I'm rejuvenated. Which will you have?" She asked, pointing to the cocoa and the champagne.

"Cocoa," Poppy said.

Elizabeth poured her a cup of steaming hot cocoa while telling Poppy this was a celebration. Poppy took a sip and studied Elizabeth's face. This was definitely a sign that she was recovering from the depression caused by Jerry's death. Poppy was thrilled that she was in such an uplifting mood, but why the mystery? What was this all about?

"Elizabeth, what's going on? You've got me in a quandary here. I'm happy to see you are happy again, but I'm unsure what you are preparing me for."

"Poppy, I got some wonderful news, and you were the first person I wanted to share it with. But then I got the call about Marley, so it had to wait. It seems only fitting that now that chapter has been put to rest, I can finally tell you my news. I had an appointment with my OB/GYN yesterday, and it was confirmed that I'm pregnant with Jerry's child."

Poppy sat stunned for a moment. This wasn't the news that she had been expecting. Oh, sure, she had reverted to her childhood, closing her eyes tight, wishing for Elizabeth's news to have a positive outcome. But this? This was great news. She knew that having Jerry's child was the tonic Elizabeth needed to move forward. She looked at Elizabeth and reached out and hugged her. Another of Poppy's wishes had come true!

"Is this a secret, Elizabeth?"

"No, not at all. I just wanted you to know first. After Jerry died, I didn't think I could love anyone. But I have found that love is unlimited; your heart expands to let others in." She had not forgotten Jerry and never would, but she had tucked that wonderful memory in a special compartment and was ready to make room for future memories with their child. Would there be someone else for her? Only time would tell, but right now, Elizabeth was happy, and nothing was going to spoil it.

Elizabeth's news gave Poppy the inspiration she needed. She was going to be twenty-seven on her next birthday. Besides

Grace, she had never had a family except her adopted one. She was not complaining. Grace and the MacHens were and would always be family. But she wanted more, and she realized she wanted it with Kurt. She closed her eyes and wished really hard!

CHAPTER 32

FOREVER AND EVER

Poppy knew what she wanted, and it was Kurt. She couldn't think of anyone else she'd rather be with. They had fun together, laughed together, and even worked well together. That was a lot of togetherness! Poppy realized she was in love with him but wasn't sure he felt the same. Oh, she knew he cared for her, but did he want to make their relationship more permanent? Were his feelings that strong? Hers definitely were. She shook off the nerves and decided there was no time like the present. Today, she would find out how she would spend the rest of her life. Had her wish come true?

Poppy hesitated before dialing his number, second-guessing herself. What if he wasn't ready or wasn't interested? Would it spoil the relationship they now had? Should she just sit back and let their relationship flow as it had been? Or risk ruining what they had? There were so many questions going through Poppy's mind. She decided to go ahead and make that call. After all, had never been timid. She proved that when she was thirteen years old, she survived by herself in the woods for ten days by stealing eggs and cooking them over a campfire. Her mind was made up. Poppy made the call and was surprised that Kurt answered before the phone even rang. Before she could get a word out, he told her he just was dialing her number. He was calling to ask if she would like to come to the ranch for supper. Of course, she would. She told Kurt yes.

Poppy arrived around 6:30, and Kurt greeted her at the front door. He steered her into the dining room, where there were flowers everywhere. She looked at him in amazement as he pulled her chair back for her to sit down. Was this some type of celebration? Had she missed an anniversary of something? First date? First kiss? No, she would remember that. She didn't care what it was, she was loving it! Their conversation started out light but turned serious when she shared Elizabeth's baby news. Kurt dropped his fork onto his plate; he was that surprised. He was so happy for Elizabeth. She had been having a hard time since Jerry's death. But a baby? Who knew? God works in mysterious ways, he thought. Poppy knew it was the perfect opportunity to tell him how she felt. It would break her heart if he didn't feel the same way. Every time she looked at him, her knees got weak. Tonight, her knees felt like overcooked spaghetti. She never knew what people meant when they talked about getting butterflies in your stomach until she met Kurt. She was about to speak when Kurt asked if he could talk first. She smiled and nodded.

"Poppy, we have known each other for several months, and I have had many bright spots in my life, but you have been the brightest of all. You light up my path in life. Poppy, I don't think I was actually living before I met you."

Poppy sat stunned at Kurt's comment. She realized she should never have doubted his feelings.

Kurt looked directly into her eyes, then continued. "I guess I'm stepping on my tongue here. Poppy, what I'm trying to say here is: Will you marry me?" Kurt asked as he opened a ring box with a beautiful diamond ring inside.

Poppy was lost for words for a few seconds. Then she looked at him. "Kurt, when I was a little girl, I read all the books I could find. Their stories were my world. That's where I lived. The words on the pages would take me away. I would imagine that I was the heroine and my knight in shining armor would come and find me. I've always loved stories about heroes. Until Grace MacDonald adopted me, that's the way I made it through each day by reading my books and daydreaming. I used my vivid imagination to take me away from my lonely existence. Kurt, you are my dream come true, my knight, and my hero. I wished for you! I love you, and YES, I will marry you. A million times, YES."

Poppy had found her *forever* home in Vernon Parish. Who knew that when she accepted the job here, she would meet her soulmate in Kurt O'Shea? He was definitely the love of her life. And, if she hadn't come here, she would never have known she had a half-brother, Jack McKay. She was still getting used to saying, brother. The McKays had let her know she was part of the family and she was welcome at every family function. This was home!

CHAPTER 33

A PROMISE FROM THE HEART

Myles Roche was eighteen and playing basketball with his neighborhood friends when he collapsed on the basketball court. He was immediately taken to a local hospital where his uncle was a doctor. After an exam and extensive tests, it was determined that Myles suffered a heart attack, which caused permanent damage. It could be controlled for now with drugs, but that was only a temporary fix. There would be so many physical activities that he would not be able to perform on his own. He would need a heart transplant, and although his name was added to the list, it wasn't called a waiting list for nothing. Another person's name is added to the national transplant waiting list every ten minutes. Selection is based on the most urgent need for a transplant and also on who would be most likely to have the best chance of survival if the heart is transplanted. Myles and his family were ecstatic when they received the call that he was a match for the heart he desperately needed.

After his surgery, Myles realized every day what a magnificent gift he had received. He knew he had a bit of a road to recovery but felt that he should thank someone. His uncle advised him against it. As a doctor, he told him the recipient should remain anonymous for many reasons, but Myles persisted. His uncle did find out that the donor had no living relatives and passed the information on to Myles, thinking that would be the end of it. But it wasn't. Myles was saddened, thinking the donor couldn't have been all alone in this world. He must have had someone. Seeing the effect this was having on Myles, his uncle agreed to see what he could learn about the donor.

His Uncle Charles pulled through for him! The donor had a fiancé listed in the contact information, and she lived in the same state as Myles.

"Are you sure you want to do this? Contact this woman?"

Myles told his uncle it was something he felt very strongly about, and his mind was made up. He didn't want to just call her. He wanted to meet her in person! Against his better judgment, his uncle passed a piece of paper to him with the name Elizabeth Weaver, Leesville, Louisiana, written on it. He gave him the information with a warning.

"You never know, Myles, how she will receive you. If you want to do that, then I say do it. Don't be disappointed if things don't work out how you thought they would. She might find it very upsetting to know that someone she loved has his heart beating in someone else's chest."

Myles hugged him and left his office with a smile. The next step was to locate the fiancé and then talk his family into driving him there. Piece of cake, he thought.

She wasn't hard to find. Elizabeth Weaver was a U.S. Marshall serving the Vernon Parish area. He was taking his time deciding if he should go see her. He kept remembering his uncle's words. 'Things may not work out how you think they will, Miles.'

Despite his uncle's warning, this was something he had to do. His mind made up, he and his parents began the road trip to Leesville, Louisiana!

A few minutes before noon, Myles entered the Vernon Parish Sheriff's office. He approached the deputy at the front desk and asked him to direct him to Marshall Elizabeth Weaver.

The deputy looked up from his desk and answered.

"Just a minute, I'll call her office." He picked up the phone, punched in a number, and told the person at the other end they had a visitor.

"Okay, son, have a seat, and Marshall Weaver will be right out."

Myles sat on a bench in the lobby. He was nervous, and his hands were sweaty. He wondered if he was doing the right thing. Too late to turn back now. He was here, and she would be standing before him shortly. A few minutes later, Myles looked up as a young woman, tall and slim with long blond hair, approached him. She looked at the young man seated on the bench, staring at him briefly. Elizabeth didn't know him but felt she should. He was different in some strange way that she couldn't pinpoint. She looked at him briefly, then without saying a word, she motioned for him to follow her. They walked into her office, and she offered him a seat. He sat nervously in front of her desk, then looked at her and spoke.

"Ma'am, I have wanted to see you, but I wasn't sure I should. I wasn't even sure that I could," he said with a quiver in his voice. "My name is Myles. Myles Roche. My Uncle Charles told me I should send you a letter, but that was so impersonal, and to me, it was just too important not to see you in person. I wanted to thank someone for a gift I received, and you're the only one I could find," Miles said hesitantly.

Elizabeth sat speechless for a few seconds and looked at him. She saw that he was nervous and speaking with some reluctance.

Myles became uncomfortable and thought, for the first time, that his Uncle Charles was right. He had made a big mistake in coming here. He stood up to leave, but Elizabeth motioned with her hand for him to sit back down. She needed to find out what gift he was referring to.

"Myles, it's nice to meet you, but I have no idea what gift you are thanking me for. Can you tell me a little more?"

Nervously, he looked her straight in the eyes and told her the gift he was referring to was keeping him alive. Without it, he wouldn't be sitting in her office right now.

Myles saw a tear roll down her cheek. He then realized how emotional this was for her. He had not counted on this. It was emotional for him, too. Was he wrong to come here?

Elizabeth took a deep breath before asking. "You got Jerry's heart, didn't you?"

Unable to speak, Myles just nodded. He was trying desperately to hold back tears. She got up from her chair and walked around the desk. She reached out with both arms. As Myles stood up, she came closer and hugged him tightly for a few seconds. She thought she felt Jerry's heartbeat like she had so many times before. Myles wasn't sure how to respond, but he put his arms around her shoulders and hugged her back. While still embracing him in a soft voice, she asked.

"Are you going to college?"

"Yes, Ma'am, I will be. I'm enrolled at Tulane University for the fall semester."

"Will you promise me one thing, Myles?"

"Yes, Ma'am, if I can."

"Do something exceptional with your life. There's a good man's heart beating inside of you. Don't waste it."

Miles unbuttoned the top four buttons of his shirt, exposing a scar in the middle of his chest. He took Elizabeth's right hand and placed it over the scar.

"That's a promise that I will keep, Ma'am," Myles said while looking into her eyes. He released Elizabeth's hand. After Myles buttoned his shirt, he took both her hands in his and squeezed them. He released them without saying a word, turned, and walked toward the door. Then he paused and rotated to face her.

"Ma'am, can I ask you a question?"

"Sure," Elizabeth said.

"Did your Jerry like hotdogs?"

"He loved them. He ate them every chance he got. How about you?" She asked with a smile.

"Actually, I have never liked them...that is until five days after my surgery. Now, I can't get enough of them."

Elizabeth smiled. "You take care, Myles," she said as the tears were drying on her cheeks.

Myles nodded. He was glad he had made the trip. With Elizabeth's words resonating, he turned and walked out. Elizabeth stood looking at the door Miles had just walked through for a few seconds. Shoulders heaving, she returned to her desk, took a deep breath, and blankly stared down at the report she had previously been reading. Then she smiled as she thought Jerry would have liked this young man.

CHAPTER 34

THE WEDDING VOWS

Poppy and Jack had discussed in length everything the doctor and surgical staff had told them in preparation for Jack's bone marrow transplant, which was only three days away. There was no hesitation on her part, just anxiety about being in the hospital. She typically stayed very busy, so being out of commission for a few days was going to be hard for Poppy to adjust to. She had been assured that she would feel some fatigue but would return to her normal physical activity within a few weeks.

Poppy and Kurt were sitting at *Rita's Broadway Italian Restaurant* while she explained to him that it was a pretty simple procedure for the donor. Still, he appeared worried. She assured him it was similar to a blood transfusion. Poppy's cell phone rang, and she was actually happy for the interruption. Although she knew Kurt was worried about her, he was way more apprehensive than she would be if the shoe were on the other foot. Looking at the caller ID, she saw it was Elizabeth.

Poppy knew that Elizabeth had been paying the rent on Jerry's apartment since his death, but she had yet to walk through that door. So, it was no surprise to her when Elizabeth asked if she would accompany her while she sorted through his things. Elizabeth hadn't worked up the courage to go there and, even now, didn't want to approach the task alone. She knew all of Jerry's belongings had to be dealt with, but she was not sure what she wanted to keep and what she wanted to give to charity. She hoped Poppy could help her decide. Knowing how difficult it would be for Elizabeth to revisit the past, she immediately agreed.

It was before noon when Elizabeth turned the key on Jerry's apartment door. When she walked in, the first thing she saw was a picture of her and Jerry sitting on the top of an end table. But the smell, oh the smell of the apartment, gave her flashbacks of times spent with Jerry. It was almost overwhelming. She looked over at the kitchen where Jerry had cooked their first meal together and remembered the burnt spaghetti sauce; he had tried so hard to make it from scratch. Poppy put her hand on Elizabeth's arm as a calming gesture, but Elizabeth assured her she was all right. They glanced over the apartment and saw it was immaculate, with everything in its place and not a speck of dust anywhere. Poppy and Elizabeth walked into the bedroom, each carrying a box. Poppy started emptying dresser drawers, figuring they could sort through stuff later. She watched as Elizabeth walked over to the bureau, picked up a bottle of cologne, lifted it to her nose, and sniffed. She turned her head to look at Poppy. Smiling, she put the bottle in her purse. Poppy didn't blame her for wanting to hold on to the spray bottle—she knew it smelled like Jerry.

When Poppy was assured all the dresser drawers were empty, she headed for the nightstand. Opening the drawer, she saw an envelope lying on top. The handwriting on the envelope said: *Wedding Vows*. Not knowing if this find would upset Elizabeth, she hesitated while deciding whether to show it to her now or wait until later. Poppy made up her mind and called Elizabeth over, offering her the envelope with her outstretched hand. She took it from Poppy, read the inscription on the front, and held it in both hands for a moment. Without saying a word, she slowly opened the envelope, looked at Poppy, and started reading out loud:

My darling Elizabeth, you are my life and my family. I promise you that whatever life gives us, it gives us together. I pledge my unwavering support. I promise to love you always. I vow to wake up every day and choose you. I can't promise that there won't be rainy days or dark clouds, but I can promise I will always be here for you when those days come. I promise to listen to you, hold your hand, and love you forever.

Elizabeth looked over at Poppy, who expected to see tears, but this time, there were none. Elizabeth smiled, folded the paper, and placed it back into the envelope before tucking it into her purse. She felt as though she had found a treasure. She had, in fact—it was Jerry's final gift to her.

Poppy couldn't help but notice that Elizabeth had brightened and picked up her step after reading the wedding vows that Jerry had composed for her. It seemed to lighten their task, and two hours later, they were done.

"Poppy, I will leave the apartment key with you because Kurt has arranged for two ranch hands to clean the apartment out and keep whatever they could use. The rest will be donated to charity. I have everything I want to keep in these two boxes and in my purse. It doesn't seem like much, but I will cherish the items I've kept forever."

As they walked out the door, Elizabeth stopped and looked at the picture on the end table in the living room. It was a picture of the two of them standing up in a fishing boat, smiling and holding up two bass. Elizabeth had the much larger one, and Jerry's fish looked like a minnow. Picking up the picture, she kissed it and put it in one of the boxes she was holding. She paused at the door on the way out, turned, looked at the apartment, and smiled.

Poppy knew this would be Elizabeth's last visit. She would never return to this apartment.

CHAPTER 35

THE GIFT

On the day of the procedure, Jack and his family arrived at the hospital first. They took a seat as they waited to be called to the Registration desk. Jack was getting good at waiting—it seems that's all he had done for months now. Margo looked over at him, and sensing his anxiousness, she took his hand. He glanced at his mother for the look he remembered from his childhood. The facial expression that told him everything would be okay. Yes, there it was. He relaxed, smiled, and squeezed her hand. The Major looked at Jack and caught his eye. Never having been the 'mushy' type, his father just smiled and gave him a 'thumbs up'.

Ten minutes later, Poppy arrived with Kurt and Elizabeth for emotional support. The truth was that even though Poppy had assured Kurt the transplant procedure was a walk in the park, she was a little bit nervous. Hence, the reason she hadn't told Grace about this procedure. Her mother would be here in Leesville, hovering over her—which would shatter her nerves! Seeing Jack and his family, she walked over and greeted him with a "Good morning, brother."

Jack stood up and hugged her. Margo looked over at them as they were hugging. Then she looked at Poppy and mouthed 'Thank you' as a tear escaped from her eye. Poppy just nodded her head.

A nurse walked into the waiting room and asked if they were ready. This is it, Poppy thought. It's time to get the show on the road. She looked over at Kurt and gave him a warm smile. Then she and Jack got up, took each other's hand in a show of support, and followed the nurse. They were each given their own room with a curtain for privacy and quickly changed into hospital gowns. Then, they were put on gurneys and pushed out into the hallway. As they were wheeled down the corridor together, side by side, Poppy reached over, looking for Jack's hand. She found it and clasped it gently in a show of solidarity. Everyone could see them holding hands as the gurneys were being pushed, and they entered the operating room.

When the doctor entered the operating theater, he stood between Jack and Poppy's beds and explained the procedure so they would know what to expect. When he finished, he asked if they had any questions. Jack had one—when do we get started? He got his answer quickly because once the IV drip started and the lights went out, he and Poppy were fast asleep.

As Elizabeth sat in the waiting room with Kurt, she could tell by his body language that he was worried about Poppy. Maybe worried wasn't the right word, but concerned. She reached over and put her hands on Kurt's shoulder, and he turned to face her.

"Kurt, she will be fine. I'm so proud of her. She's doing the right thing."

He knew Elizabeth was right but couldn't keep himself from turning toward the operating room doors while he waited expectantly for someone to tell him that all was well. He loved Poppy with no reservations, and that was borne out today as he realized he couldn't exist without her.

Margo moved closer to the Major and looked into his eyes. He knew how worried she was about Jack. He was concerned too, but didn't show it—he wanted to be strong for Margo. Lord, how he still loved this woman. Putting his arm around her waist, he pulled her towards him.

"Emmitt, I'm sitting here admonishing myself for how I treated Poppy when she first came to Vernon Parish. I was so rude and treated her with disrespect. I'm so sorry, Emmitt. She's such a beautiful young lady, and she's saving our son."

"Margo, you don't need to apologize to me, but you should talk to Poppy and tell her how you feel. Remember, she's not only saving our son. She's saving her brother!"

Jack and Poppy awoke around the same time. The staff had put them in the same recovery room.

Poppy looked over at Jack and asked, "Are you okay?"

He smiled at her and raised his hand as if to wave. "I'm just fine, Sis."

Poppy tilted her head over to look at Jack. *"Sis..."* Poppy said. "I've never been called that before. It sounds strange; I like it."

"You will get used to it," Jack said with a soft laugh.

Poppy reached over and took Jack's hand, gave it a weak squeeze, and said, "I love you, brother." Then she dozed off to sleep.

Kurt's time staring at the operating room doors paid off after a couple of hours. Of course, to him, it seemed like an eternity before the doctor came to the waiting room to speak to the family. He first addressed the McKays and assured them that Jack had come through the procedure like a champ and would heal fast. He assured them that they would closely check his blood cell count, but he wasn't expecting any issues. Then he looked at Kurt and Elizabeth.

"Poppy is doing fine. She should be back at full speed in about two weeks. Jack is fortunate that she not only matched but also stepped up and offered to be a donor. Seeing them together, I couldn't help but notice their strong bond. Their relationship represents the definition of familial love. They are lucky to have each other."

CHAPTER 36

OUR WISH FOR YOU

Poppy got off work on a Friday evening and decided to stroll through the cold night air. She turned up the fleece collar of her coat to fit snugly around her neck as she walked down Third Street toward the courthouse. Her hands stung from the cold when she placed them in her coat pocket. Poppy was caught up in her thoughts as she walked down the sidewalk. Suddenly, the flash of bright lights interrupted her reminiscing. She noticed the decorative Christmas lights illuminating the night while the courthouse's street lamps had been dimmed to highlight the Christmas décor. She had no particular destination in mind as she strolled down the street. Her goal was to enjoy the sights and sounds of her new hometown. She was thinking back on all that had transpired since she left the mountains of Georgia and arrived in Leesville, Louisiana. Poppy couldn't help but think how different her life was now. Six months ago, she met a family she didn't know existed and discovered a rich family history. From what she had learned, listing her family's accomplishments could fill a history book. She held up her left hand and admired the ring that had just been placed there by the man she planned to spend the rest of her life with. Looking up, she realized she was standing in front of the twenty-foot-tall Christmas Tree on the courthouse lawn. Next to the tree was a nativity scene that she was told came alive with real people and animals on Christmas Eve. Poppy took a seat on a park bench facing the tree. She closed her eyes and could picture the nativity scene as it would appear in just a few short days with Mary, Joseph, baby Jesus, sheep, goats, and a donkey.

While looking up at the angel on top of the tree, a little girl approached the bench and sat beside her. The frosty night air had turned the girl's cheeks a rosy red. She was bundled up with a scarf, a knit cap was pulled down over her auburn hair and ears, and wool mittens covered her hands. She smiled as she looked at Poppy.

"Are you Ms. Poppy Nichols?" The child asked.

Poppy looked over at her and smiled. "Yes, how do you know my name?"

"Everyone knows you, Ms. Nichols," the child said.

"Since you know my name, will you tell me yours?"

"It's Lucy."

They both turned their attention back to the angel on the top of the tree.

Without looking away, the little girl asked, "Do you believe in angels, Ms. Nichols?"

Poppy paused for a minute, thinking it was an odd question, or was it? "Let me ask you a question, Lucy. Do you believe in angels?"

"Yes, yes, ma'am, I do," The little girl replied.

"Then that makes two of us, Lucy," Poppy said, returning her gaze to the angel on the top of the Christmas tree. "That's a beautiful bracelet that you have on your wrist. I bet someone who loves you very much must have given that to you."

"Yes, Ma'am, my dad did just before he died; he's an angel now," Lucy said quietly with her head bowed.

"I can see why you believe in angels," Poppy said with a smile. Poppy heard a woman's voice call for the little girl.

"Lucy, it's time to go."

Lucy turned her attention away from the angel and looked at Poppy. "Merry Christmas, Ms. Nichols," and ran off to join her mother.

"Merry Christmas, Lucy," Poppy replied softly. Then, she lifted herself off the bench and headed to the sidewalk. She tucked her hands inside her coat pockets and turned into the cold north wind as she headed to her truck. Poppy stopped and turned, taking one last look at the Christmas tree and the angel on top. She smiled and then walked off into the night.

When Poppy returned home, she was glad for the warmth her cozy living room offered. She took off her coat, sat on the couch, and closed her eyes. So much had happened since she accepted a job in a city she had never seen before. If she hadn't found her cousin Elizabeth, she's not sure she would have taken that leap of faith and moved to Vernon Parish. But once here, nothing could drag her away. Yes, there had been tragedy on the Sabine River, but like all the rest, the river was in her blood now. She reflected on what her cousin, Jeff Simmons, had said the first time they met. The Sabine was like a well-rehearsed orchestra. It drew her like a siren's song that only the river could play. It was like an old tune from long ago that had manifested from a dream without hearing the composition, and she knew every note. The river seemed to play for her and only her. It spoke a language she had never heard before, but she understood every word. Along with the Burr Ferry Community, it pulled her like a magnet. But somehow, it was more than that; it was a feeling she couldn't explain, but it was there, and it was strong. She had matured quickly in her job and herself, developing wisdom beyond her years. She'd also had some notable accomplishments since her arrival. She remembered what Sheriff Mitchell Newman had said, *'I have known Rufus Lewis for over forty years, and I've never seen old Rufus smile. He's worn a scowl on his face like a badge of honor. But Poppy, you made him smile.'* Poppy would never forget what Pastor Tilley had said once in Sunday school. *'Will you leave a legacy? What will people remember about you? What will your family members say? What will you be known for? If you don't like the course your life has taken, it *isn't too late to change it.'* Yes, she thought she was making a difference. Poppy leaned back on the sofa and looked at the end table next to the couch. She placed her hand on her mother's journal and ran her fingers over its old, cracked leather cover. She wished her parents hadn't died before she was old enough to know them. Maybe if she wished really hard, she could remember them. No, that was for little girls, but she closed her eyes and wished anyway. With her hand still on the journal, she took a deep breath and closed her eyes; she soon drifted off to sleep.

Poppy's eyes had been shut for only a moment when she heard a rustling in the kitchen. She opened her eyes and saw a slim man with dark hair and an attractive woman walk into the living room. She stared straight ahead at them and realized it was her parents standing before her. They had soft, sweet smiles, and a warm, radiant glow surrounded them.

"We are proud of you, Poppy. This is where you were meant to be. My hope for you is that you will find the happiness your dad and I found. Our wish is that your fiancée feels the same for you as you do for him and that you have children to love the same way we love you. You are going to do great things with your life. The hardships you endured in your first thirteen years were difficult, but they have molded you into the loving and compassionate woman you are today. You are a beautiful young lady, making a difference to everyone you touch. These are your people, and Vernon Parish is your home; take care of them, Poppy," Abby Nichols said.

Her father looked at her and smiled.

"You were put here for a reason, Poppy, and you have made us proud. You have been blessed to have this position of protection and leadership. Always see the joy in this wonderful life. And when children come, hold them close when they are scared and teach them right from wrong. Follow your heart, and you will make the right decisions. The thought of you gives us hope that the world can be a better place," Louis Nichols said.

Poppy watched as her mother took a pink ribbon from her hair and her father took off his wedding ring. Her mother also removed her wedding band, ran the ribbon through both rings, and secured them in a bow.

Poppy opened her eyes and looked around the living room. She saw no one but could swear she had not been alone. Was it a dream? It seemed so natural. She had seen her parents as they had so lovingly been described to her by other family members. She smiled and lifted herself off the couch. Looking at the clock on the mantle it read 6:30 a.m. Well, that was some dream, she thought. Poppy had slept the entire night on the couch. Remembering the dream, she looked over at her mother's journal. Laying on top of it was a beautiful pink ribbon with two wedding rings intertwined and tied in a bow. She picked up the rings and held them tight, clutching them to her heart and smiling. Had her wish come true?

"Thanks, Mom and Dad, for giving me such a lovely family. I love you."

Poppy's phone was lying on the coffee table when it rang. She looked at the caller ID and saw it was Kurt. She answered with a smile, "Hello, Kurt."

"Poppy, are you up for an early breakfast? I could hardly sleep last night. There's so much I want to talk to you about. I had the strangest, and well...most wonderful dream. I want to tell you about it," Kurt said in an excited voice.

"Did your dream have to do with our future and children?"

"Well, yes, it did," Kurt answered curiously. "How did you know?"

She smiled to herself and then replied, "I'll explain at breakfast. I can be ready in fifteen minutes."

She laid the phone down on the table and couldn't remove the smile from her face. She knew that life with Kurt would be amazing, and this was only the beginning of her story!

EPILOGUE – DAY OF RECKONING

Four weeks after the trial started, the defense rested its case and presented closing arguments. The jury was then sent to ponder the innocence or guilt of Marley Powell. They were out only six hours before returning with a verdict. The defendant was standing in front of Judge Barton Jones. Judge Jones had presided over many murder cases and was a by-the-book judge who didn't put up with courtroom shenanigans. Poppy and Elizabeth were sitting behind District Attorney Timothy O'Connor, who personally prosecuted the case.

Judge Jones looked at the jury and then the jury foreman. "Mr. Foreman, have you reached a verdict in this case?"

The foreman spoke up loudly. "Yes, we have Your Honor."

The bailiff went to the jury foreman, took the verdict from his hand, and brought it to the judge. Jones read the verdict and handed it back to the bailiff.

The judge then looked at the foreman and asked, "What say you?"

"Your Honor, we find the defendant guilty of murder in the first degree, guilty of ten counts of racketeering, guilty of conspiracy to commit murder, guilty of twenty counts of grand theft in the second degree, guilty of interstate flight to avoid prosecution, guilty of six counts of a felon in possession of a firearm.

"Thank you, sir. You and the jury are excused," the Judge pronounced.

Elizabeth gripped Poppy's hand and smiled.

Judge Jones asked the defendant to rise so he could pronounce sentencing.

"You have been found guilty of heinous crimes as laid out in the jury verdict, which are punishable by death. It is the order of this court that you be taken to the state prison, and there, you will await your execution date. Do you have anything to say?"

Marley bowed his head and shook it.

"Bailiff, remove this man from my courtroom and ready him for transport."

The courtroom was quiet as Marley exited the court in shackles. He shuffled within a few feet of Elizabeth and Poppy with ankle chains clanking. He glanced at Elizabeth but made little eye contact. She stared back at him without blinking. The

Marley Powell ordeal had ended, and she was moving on. There was a life growing inside of her—a little girl that Jerry would never get to see. But Elizabeth vowed that she would raise her in a way that would make Jerry proud.

Poppy reached over and squeezed Elizabeth's hand, then whispered, "Justice has been served."

ABOUT THE AUTHOR

Michael W. Mitcham is a retired law enforcement officer and a U.S. Navy veteran from the Vietnam War Era. Born in Leesville, Louisiana, and reared in the Burr Ferry community, Mike spent his childhood balancing school and work on his family farm. This farm inspired his autobiography, *Life on Old Sand Road*, a book of short stories describing his life from birth to deployment. Following his service, Mike moved to Tampa, Florida, and began his career in law enforcement. Today, Mike spends his retirement writing poetry and romantic fiction, drawing much of his inspiration from his life. His debut book was titled *Bird on a Wire*, followed by *Charlotte MacHen: Angel on Fire*. Next in the series is *Charlotte MacHen: My Daughters' Keeper*, and the final installment in his Charlotte MacHen series, *Charlotte MacHen: Yellow Scarf*. Mike can be contacted at michaelwmitcham@gmail.com. His books are available on Amazon.com

Made in the USA
Columbia, SC
14 March 2024